THE FORTUNES OF TEXAS

*Follow the lives and loves of a complex family
with a rich history and deep ties
in the Lone Star State*

DIGGING FOR SECRETS

A ruse brings six estranged Fortunes to Chatelaine, Texas, to supposedly have their most secret wishes granted. They're thrilled—until they discover someone is seeking vengeance for a long-ago wrong...and turning their lives upside down!

Fortune's Convenient Cinderella

Bear Fortune had sworn off love—forever. So when Morgana Wells catches his eye, he's got an unconventional proposal: become the mother of his child! Housekeeper Morgana's got her own reasons for being intrigued by the Fortunes...and her position as a motel maid is the way to find out more about them. But will the secrets she discovers about them *both* shatter any hope of a shared future?

Dear Reader,

Welcome back to the exciting world of The Fortunes of Texas! I have always wanted to write a *Cinderella*-inspired book, and this story about Barrington "Bear" Fortune and Morgana Mills was so much fun to write. There aren't any talking animals, but I am curious to hear how many nods to the original fairy tale you discover while reading.

Bear is a wealthy oilman who stays away from his family for months at a time, but when he hears that his brother is alive after years in hiding, he travels to Chatelaine, Texas, to see him. He didn't expect to be so drawn to the beautiful maid who sings and dances while cleaning his room at the old motor lodge on the edge of town. Morgana is reluctant to share any personal details, but she sure has been asking a lot of questions about the Fortune family. He is determined to find out what she's hiding, and learns some interesting facts. Bear is a pro when it comes to closing million-dollar business deals, so why is he having such a hard time convincing Morgana to go along with a proposal that will benefit them both?

I hope you enjoy *Fortune's Convenient Cinderella*. As always, thank you for reading!

Best wishes,

Makenna Lee

FORTUNE'S CONVENIENT CINDERELLA

MAKENNA LEE

Harlequin

THE FORTUNES OF TEXAS

Special thanks and acknowledgment are given to
Makenna Lee for her contribution to
The Fortunes of Texas: Digging for Secrets miniseries.

Recycling programs
for this product may
not exist in your area.

H Harlequin®
THE FORTUNES
OF TEXAS

ISBN-13: 978-1-335-59485-3

Fortune's Convenient Cinderella

Harlequin Enterprises ULC
22 Adelaide St. West, 41st Floor
Toronto, Ontario M5H 4E3, Canada
www.Harlequin.com

Printed in Lithuania

MIX
Paper | Supporting
responsible forestry
FSC® C021394

Makenna Lee is an award-winning romance author living in the Texas Hill Country with her real-life hero and their two children, one of whom has Down syndrome and inspired her first Harlequin book, *A Sheriff's Star*. She writes heartwarming contemporary romance that celebrates real-life challenges and the power of love and acceptance. She has been known to make people laugh and cry in the same book. Makenna is often drinking coffee with a cat on her lap while writing, reading or plotting a new story. Her wish is to write stories that touch your heart, making you feel, think and dream.

Books by Makenna Lee

The Fortunes of Texas: Digging for Secrets

Fortune's Convenient Cinderella

Harlequin Special Edition

The Women of Dalton Ranch

The Rancher's Love Song
Her Secret to Keep

Home to Oak Hollow

A Sheriff's Star
In the Key of Family
A Child's Christmas Wish
A Marriage of Benefits
Lessons in Fatherhood
The Bookstore's Secret

The Fortunes of Texas: Hitting the Jackpot

Fortune's Fatherhood Dare

Visit the Author Profile page
at Harlequin.com for more titles.

To Mackenzie.
We are so glad you've become part of our lives.
Thanks for making our son so happy!

Chapter One

A talented female voice singing ABBA's "Dancing Queen" made Barrington "Bear" Fortune smile before he'd even unlocked his motel room door—with an actual metal key. The pretty maid he'd seen around the old motor lodge was standing on the foot of his bed, barefoot and on top of a pile of stripped-off sheets. She stretched to swipe her duster across the ceiling, and her knee-length white skirt swished around her slim legs as her hips swayed to the upbeat song.

Something warmed inside Bear's chest. He squeezed the key in one hand and his laptop case with the other, all in an effort to resist pulling her into his arms just to see what kind of dance partner this alluring and mysterious woman would be.

The door swung closed with a thud, and as she spun to face him, her feet slipped out from under her. She landed on her butt, bounced off the mattress and right into a standing position at the foot of the bed.

He chuckled, surprising himself with the sound of his own laugh because he hadn't heard it in months. "Wow. Impressive move."

"Mr. Fortune, I am so sorry! I don't usually stand on the bed, but there was a cobweb. Way up high." She stepped into a pair of black ballerina flats and smoothed the front of her uniform, a white cotton dress that buttoned up the front. A turquoise apron with big pockets was tied around her slim waist.

"It's fine. I was just jumping on the bed this morning," he said with a straight face. A skill he'd perfected while making business deals around the world.

Her eyes widened even further at his joke, and she worked her mouth, but nothing came out.

"Kidding," he said, then added, "Maybe."

That made her smile, and it lit up her face. Long, dark eyelashes feathered around eyes the color of vibrant rainforest moss, and a lush mouth that had caught his attention the very first time he saw her coming out of a motel room was quivering with a smile she was holding back.

"Once again, I'm sorry, Mr. Fortune."

"You don't have to call me Mr. Fortune. Please, call me Bear." He gave her one of his trademark grins that often made women giggle, or on occasion, give a kittenish purr of invitation. But this young woman only ducked her head.

"Bear. Got it. I'm Morgana. I'll be done in here in a few minutes." She scooped up the pile of sheets from the foot of the bed. "Or do you want me to come back later?"

"Now is fine. Take your time." He was alone so often and usually liked it that way, but having her in his room was… He couldn't put a finger on the feeling stirring inside him, but he wanted her around. The entertainment possibilities of having her in his room were intriguing. He put his laptop case on the bistro-sized table by the window. "And feel free to keep singing."

A rosy blush spread across her high cheekbones. "I can't believe you heard that."

"And I enjoyed it."

She tried to hide a smile as she stuffed the sheets into a canvas bag attached to her rolling cart. "This job can get a bit monotonous. Sometimes I have to entertain myself."

"I can understand that." He was enough of a lone wolf to be well acquainted with the art of entertaining oneself. He had years of practice and had taught himself to be okay with having no one else around.

Whether from desertion, death or deceit, each person who'd disappeared from his life had made him withdraw from emotional attachments a little more each time.

Tension gathered deep in his chest, just like it always did when he thought about his ex-wife, but he pushed it away in a well-practiced move. She and his former best friend had served him a large helping of harsh reality, proving being alone and keeping love out of the equation was the safest path.

Bear sat in one of two chairs that were molded out of yellow plastic with flecks of silver. Very retro and surprisingly comfortable. He pulled out his computer and opened a new oil lease contract he needed to read before tomorrow, but his mind kept wandering back to the pretty maid moving gracefully around his small motel room.

What was Morgana's story? Why was this beautiful young woman working in a motel? Was she a loner like him, or was there something more to her story? His family had warned him that Morgana had been asking a lot of questions about the Fortune family, the mysterious Freya Fortune—who was staying in this same motel—and the silver mine collapse sixty something years ago that killed fifty miners. Fifty-one if the two mysterious notes about there being a fifty-first miner were to be believed.

His siblings and cousins had moved to Chatelaine at Freya Fortune's request. Freya might be like a beloved step-granny to some of the Fortune family, but Bear felt like something was off about her. And he had no interest in her wish granting. His brother Camden's girlfriend, who was a journalist, also suspected Freya was hiding something. Maybe even playing a cat and mouse game with the Fortune grandchildren of Edgar and Elias Fortune.

But there was no denying that Freya *had* been making their wishes and dreams come true with the money from her late husband's will, and despite some ups and downs, all his siblings and cousins were happy and in love. It was all so confusing, especially with Morgana in the mix, but it was a riddle he planned to solve before leaving town.

With the alluring maid still in the room putting clean sheets on his bed, he couldn't concentrate. All he could think about was wrinkling those sheets… with her. He gave up on getting any work done and closed his laptop.

"Where are you from?" he asked Morgana.

Her hand paused momentarily as she smoothed the ivory bedspread. "Tennessee."

"Nashville?"

"No. A little farming community that no one has ever heard of."

"A country girl. So what brought you all the way to Chatelaine, Texas?"

"Oh, I forgot to give you fresh towels." She rushed into the bathroom with a stack of fluffy white towels from her cart.

Her evasive move made him even more curious. Morgana might be fond of asking questions, but her quick retreat into the bathroom suggested she didn't like to answer them. Intriguing and just the kind of challenge he enjoyed getting to the bottom of. And speaking of bottoms, hers had moved so enticingly as she danced. Could Morgana be the distraction he'd been looking for or was she a test of his willpower? They did say keep your enemies closer. But was she *really* an enemy?

That's exactly what he intended to find out.

He glanced around his room. At first, he'd been shocked by the pink tub, sink and old square tiles, but he kind of liked the old motor lodge with its dated but not worn-out furnishings, and thanks to this entertaining maid, it was always clean. Since he'd made millions off his oil wells and by inventing drilling equipment, he'd become so used to luxury that one might think he'd snub these simple surroundings. But something about this place felt authentic in a way he'd forgotten, proving to himself that he wasn't completely jaded or spoiled by wealth.

Did he like a fine bottle of scotch, a suit tailored just for him and handmade Lucchese boots? Absolutely. But that didn't mean he couldn't appreciate the simpler things in life. And the Chatelaine Motel was the only lodging in town, so there was that. He'd had offers to stay with some of his family members, but he declined because he needed his orderly space and the quiet of being the only person in the room. However, he wasn't going to complain about the occasional singing maid being tossed into the mix.

Morgana breezed back into the room. "I ended up in town because my car broke down while I was on a road trip," she said as if there hadn't been a long pause in their conversation. "I stayed here at the motel while I waited for it to get fixed, and the owner, Hal Appleby, offered me this job. So, I decided to stay in town for a while." Her eyes darted to his for a moment. "What about you? What brought you to Chatelaine?"

"I came to see my brothers."

"Camden and West Fortune?" she asked.

"Those are the ones."

She fingered the small silver charm resting in the hollow of her throat. "West is the one who is back from the dead, right?"

"Yes."

Believing West was dead not long after his ugly divorce had put him into a downward spiral. Bear had started spending all of his time around strangers who didn't know anything about his past. He'd thrown himself into work and little else. Having his little brother back in his life was an unexpected gift that had begun to mend a small part of his damaged heart, but it would never be fully healed.

"I'm happy for your family," she said. "I can understand why you've come for an extended visit."

"I'm also working on a new business deal," he confided to distract himself from his own thoughts. "Then I'll be on my way to somewhere else far away."

Morgana cut another quick glance his way then refocused on meticulously organizing tiny bottles of bath products on her cart. "So, has Freya asked you about your biggest wish like she did with all the others?"

"You know about that?"

"Small town," she said by way of explanation. Rounding the bed, she fluffed a pillow, pulled something from one of her pockets and placed a foil-wrapped chocolate on top, but she still wouldn't fully meet his gaze. "What wish will she be granting for you?"

He ground his back teeth. Nobody went to this much trouble to give away money without gaining something in return. He barely knew Freya Fortune, the cagey woman who was claiming to be their step-grandma, but he had a strong hunch she was up to something. "I'm not interested in Freya's wish granting. Why are you asking me about it?"

"Just making conversation." She hurriedly opened the motel room door. "I'll get out of your way. Have a good afternoon."

"You, too."

She still wouldn't meet his eyes as she backed out of the open doorway, and when the wheels of her cart got caught, she gave an extra tug to get them to bump over the threshold. A roll of toilet paper tumbled off and unfurled as it rolled across the room.

She mumbled something under her breath that sounded suspiciously like damning all toilet paper to hell, and he fought a laugh he figured she wouldn't appreciate. Because the beautiful maid was trapped outside by her unwieldy cart, he snatched the roll up off the tan carpet.

"Think I'll just keep this."

"Excellent choice," she said, as if complimenting his selection of wine with dinner.

His lips twitched, and his mood that had started to sour when she'd asked about Freya's wish granting was once again lifting. This lovely young woman with her singing and dancing and unplanned humor might be up to something, but she was also good for his mood.

"See you around, dancing queen."

Chapter Two

Morgana Wells—currently using the last name Mills—rushed away from Barrington Fortune's motel room, the metal wheels of her housekeeping cart squeaking and clacking along the wooden planks of the second-floor walkway that ran across the front of the Chatelaine Motel. First, she'd been caught singing and dancing on his bed. Then she'd finished off her ill-timed performance with a roll of runaway toilet paper.

Way to completely and totally embarrass yourself.

Her face was flaming, and the blasting July 1 sun wasn't helping. The rural farm community where she'd grown up in Tennessee was in a valley near the mountains and had milder summers. This Texas heat took some getting used to. She glanced back at the door of his corner room. Kind of like the challenge of resisting Barrington's magnetism.

"Bear," she whispered. The nickname suited him. When he'd looked at her with smoldering eyes the color of the most decadent chocolate, her insides had gotten all warm and tingly. And that devilish smile…

She turned away and shook her head out of the clouds. Those same eyes had flared with warning when she'd asked what wish Freya would be granting for him. Something about the question had set him off, and she needed to find out why. It could be an important clue.

Way to push things too far too fast.

She'd been looking for a chance to talk to him and see what he knew about Freya Fortune and what information he might have to aid in her search for her grandmother, Gwenyth Wells. But she'd rushed things and he'd become defensive. Maybe she should ask her coworker, Rhonda, to clean his room from now on.

Her stomach did a little flip. She immediately dismissed that idea. The whole reason she was in Chatelaine was to gather information that would lead to putting her family back together. She just needed to go about things with a little more…*finesse*.

Morgana returned the cart to the storage room above the office that was centered below her on the ground floor. The old motor lodge sat at the tail end of Main Street, a bit removed from the action. It had fourteen rooms with decor that was stuck somewhere between the 1970s and 1980s. She had asked her boss about doing some updates, but guests seemed to like its back in time vibe, so he only made repairs rather than remodeling.

She opened the washing machine to start a load of laundry, and when she pulled out the sheets that she had stripped off Bear's bed, she caught the scent of his cologne and pulled his pillowcase to her nose. Notes of cedar mixed with cinnamon and fresh mountain air made her whole body sing in the best way possible, and she wanted more of the delicious feeling he roused. She had the inappropriate urge to take the pillowcase to her room but stuffed it into the washer instead.

There was another reason she wanted to be the one who cleaned his room. The intensely curious way he'd looked at her made her feel alive in a way she'd never known. He had the air of a man who knew the meaning of the word *passion*. And how to make a woman feel desirable. Morgana shivered.

Bear's charm gave her a pleasantly warm and tingly kind of glow, with none of the usual signs that a guy was putting on a performance with less than chivalrous intentions. It was true that she hardly knew Bear, and she might be only twenty-five years old, but she'd always been able to sense when a guy was bad news. Her mom had set a good example over the years, never letting a man push her in a direction she didn't want to go.

Bear also had a wicked sense of humor. That was one big thing checked off her list of attractive qualities—along with the butterflies and tingles, of course. And she had little doubt he knew his way around a woman's body. But how did he treat a woman when they weren't in the throes of passion? There was a charisma about him that made her want to climb back onto his bed and test that theory, and this time rumple the sheets…with *him*.

"Absolutely the worst idea you have ever had," she mumbled to herself.

They were from such completely different worlds. Bear Fortune wore designer clothes, drove a luxury car that she didn't even recognize the emblem for, and she'd heard a rumor that he had a private plane. She, on the other hand, cleaned people's rooms, shopped at thrift stores, had an old red car that had faded to orange and barely ran, and she'd never even been on an airplane, private or otherwise. They might as well be Cinderella and the prince—without the chance of a happily-ever-after in a castle.

Morgana got all the laundry started and passed by Bear's room on her way to the stairs. She paused briefly as if he might sense her presence and fling open the door and invite her inside.

I'm being completely ridiculous.

She hurriedly took the stairs and collected what she needed from the downstairs storage room. Next on the list was Freya Fortune's room. She had asked the other maid if she could always be the one who cleaned Freya's room by using the excuse that she'd bonded with Freya's orange cat. It was true that she loved seeing the cat, Sunset, but there was way more to it.

She knocked on Freya's door and waited only a few seconds before the eighty-something-year-old woman answered, dressed in a pale pink linen dress, her ash-blond hair styled into a sleek bob that brushed her jawline, and carrying one of her designer purses that matched her shoes. She was classy from head to toe. If she had told people she'd been a Hollywood movie star back in the day, most of them would have believed her.

"Perfect timing. I have an appointment," the old woman said and rushed away before Morgana could get out a single word.

"Have a nice day, Mrs. Fortune," Morgana called after her.

The woman was forever dodging her at every single turn. She was being very secretive and it was so frustrating. More and more each day, she was convinced that Freya had information she needed in her search for the grandmother she'd never met.

What is Freya hiding?

She winced because she herself was being deceptive, but she meant no harm to anyone. Morgana was on a mission to reunite her family and solve the mystery surrounding the 1965 silver mine collapse. No one could know her true identity. Not yet.

And as far as locating her estranged grandmother, she'd been impossible to find. It's like she dropped off the face of the earth.

The cat rushed over to see her, and she picked him up, not caring that she'd have cat hair on her clothes. "How are you today, Sunset?"

The animal rubbed his fluffy head against Morgana's cheek and his purr motor revved to full speed. She cuddled him for a moment longer before getting to work. Once a week, she gave their extended-stay guest's room a deep cleaning, and the other days she just gave it a quick once-over and freshened the towels. Today was a full cleaning, which is probably why Freya had ducked out so quickly. She only stayed around when Morgana was doing something that wouldn't take more than a few minutes.

She started in the kitchenette area. It was a perk Freya had in her room that she and Bear did not. But if you were going to live in a motor lodge motel, she supposed it was a must. Freya had bought a fancy coffee maker and dishes much cuter than the plain white ones the motel provided. They were French blue with delicate white flowers around the edge. She had also replaced the old standard ivory curtains with raw silk ones in an icy blue and the bedspread was sapphire with throw pillows that matched the curtains. Morgana's eyes drifted across the room and landed on the bookshelf that was filled with an impressive number of classic novels and a small collection of thimbles. But there was no other sign that the old woman liked to sew. The thimbles made her think of her own mother who could use a sewing machine to create anything she set her mind to—including most of the clothes Morgana had worn while growing up on the farm.

Over the past few months, she thought Freya would finally reveal something that would help her discover what became of her grandmother. Freya had to have picked up some piece of useful information from her deceased husband, Elias Fortune. He must've disclosed something to her over the years, but so far, she claimed to know nothing.

At first, the widow seemed to be doing good deeds but slowly Morgana had begun to wonder if Freya had an alternative motive that wasn't so altruistic. From previous conversations with her new friend Haley, the reporter also had similar suspicions about Freya's reasons for being in Chatelaine. There was just something about the whole situation that didn't make sense, but she couldn't pin down exactly what it was.

Once she was done cleaning, Morgana came out of Freya's room just as the other maid, Rhonda, stepped from a room down the way. "Are you finished for the day?"

Rhonda swiped the back of her hand dramatically across her forehead. "Yes, thank goodness. This last room was a doozy. Beer cans and fast-food trash everywhere. I hate it when someone has a drinking party in their room."

"At least they weren't loud. Since my room is right above that one, I would know," Morgana said about her comped second-floor room. A benefit of working here for less pay than Rhonda was because the sweet, brassy divorcée lived in a small apartment in town.

The woman looked at her watch. "I have to get home and shower. I have an appointment to get my roots dyed before my date tonight." She touched her bottle blond hair that was currently twisted into a bun.

"Who's the lucky man?"

"Remember the guy I told you about who I met at Cowgirl Café? He saw me in GreatStore and asked me out."

"That's wonderful! Have fun on your hot date tonight."

"Oh, I plan to. We're having dinner at the Chatelaine Bar and Grill and then after that..." Her middle-aged coworker waggled her eyebrows while fanning her face. "Who knows. I'll see you tomorrow, kid."

Morgana chuckled and waved before going into the small office where the motor lodge's owner, Hal Appleby, was click-clacking away on his ancient computer. She'd finally talked her mom into getting a laptop, and she was working on doing the same for Hal, but he was resistant and frequently muttered about newfangled technology. The sixtysomething widower was a great boss. Kind, generous and always willing to help out a friend.

"All the rooms are clean and ready for the next guests."

"That's great." He brushed his hand through his thinning gray hair. "We just got a reservation for two rooms for tomorrow. I'm going to put them in rooms three and four."

"Good choice. Did you have fun on your date last night?"

He shook his head and tried not to smile, but his cheeks were turning ruddy. "It wasn't a date. Just dinner with an old friend who has moved back to town."

"If you say so. I think she's a lovely lady and you

shouldn't rule it out." Morgana sighed inwardly. It seemed like everyone was dating, except her.

The lobby door swung open, and a young couple came inside, so she excused herself and went back upstairs to her room. Only two doors down from Bear's. Hers was smaller than Freya's room with a real kitchenette, but using odds and ends, Morgana had turned one corner into her own version of a kitchen. Hal had kindly provided her with a mini fridge, hot plate, toaster oven and the plain white dishes Freya wasn't using. She was so thankful for all of it. The mini fridge sat on the floor under a garage sale table, and the other items were arranged on top.

Like her mom had taught her, she'd sanded and painted the table. The top was a soothing shade of blue with whimsical little fairies dancing up the tapered sage-green legs. When it was time to leave Chatelaine, she would try to sell the table for more than the few dollars she'd paid for it.

She made a mental note to keep an eye out for furniture that had been set out in front of houses on trash day. It was amazing to see the kind of things people tossed out. Refinishing and repurposing found items is how her mom had made extra money when times got tough—which had happened often. Following in her footsteps, she would fix up a few pieces and save the money. With a little extra cash, she could afford to get her car repaired properly and quit just throwing temporary fixes at it.

Morgana took a quick shower like she always did

after she finished work for the day and then settled in to read *Cinderella Stories from Around the World.* The book had been left behind by a guest, and she was waiting to see if they wanted it mailed back to them. Hal had chuckled when she'd told him she was going to take the book to her room and read it, but fairy tales had been a love of hers for as long as she could remember. She knew the fantastical stories weren't true to life. The perfectly tied-up-with-a-bow happy endings weren't something you could very often expect to happen, but as she saw it, a girl had to dream.

By early evening, Morgana finished the last Cinderella story. This one had been from the country of Germany. And now, she was hungry for something more than what was in her room, and she was too keyed up to lie around and watch TV. She needed to get out of these four walls, and she knew just the thing. A sweet woman who'd been a guest a few weeks ago had struck up a conversation with her about books, and when she'd checked out, she'd left Morgana a twenty-five-dollar Remi's Reads gift card as a tip. She'd been waiting to use it during the July Fourth sale they were having this week.

Morgana stepped out of her room at the same time Bear was coming out of his. Of course, her heart rate took off like the rapid pace of a hummingbird's wings. "Hey, neighbor," she said and locked her door.

He looked between her and the room she'd just

come out of with her leather backpack purse over one shoulder. "Do you live here at the motel?"

A tickle of embarrassment swirled through her, and she tugged on the midthigh hem of her favorite periwinkle-and-white sundress but quickly reminded herself that she had nothing to be embarrassed about. There were several reasons Morgana had taken the job as a maid at the old motor lodge. One, because she was from out of town and needed a place to stay and the position came with a small single room. But more importantly, because Freya lived here. Morgana thought proximity would help develop a relationship. And now, having Bear Fortune staying at the motel, it was another good reason to remain here a little longer.

"Yes, I'm living here temporarily. It's a perk of working here."

"That's convenient. Where are you headed?"

She dropped her keys into her purse. "I need a new book because I finished the one I was reading. *Cinderella Stories from Around the World.* I'll be happy to let you borrow it," she said, testing to see if his sense of humor really was as good as she suspected.

He grinned. "Thanks, but I've already read that one."

She couldn't hide her smile. "I'm walking to Remi's Reads. It's a bookstore."

"I've been there. My cousin Linc Fortune and his wife Remi own it."

"Oh, that's right. There really are a lot of Fortunes around town." They started walking, and he followed her down the stairs.

"That's kind of far to be walking, isn't it?"

Morgana shrugged and rubbed the star charm on her necklace, like she tended to do when she was nervous. She didn't want to admit that her car wasn't running—again—and she didn't have the money to fix it yet. Maybe she shouldn't be spending money on books, but they were one of the few pleasures she afforded herself. "The walk saves me from having to get a gym membership."

"I'm going over to my brother West's house, and I'm happy to give you a ride to the bookstore if you want. It's on my way."

She hesitated but only long enough to remember she'd been looking for an excuse to get a closer look at his vehicle. The sleek silver car made her think of the magical coach that took Cinderella to the royal ball, and her little faded orange car was more like the pumpkin, sad and broken on the side of the road. Very fitting that she and her mom had actually named her car Pumpkin. At least once, she wanted to be the one who was riding in the extravagant coach.

"A ride would be nice. Thank you for the offer."

"You're welcome."

Morgana walked beside him but neither of them spoke. This would also be another chance to see if he knew anything to help with her search for her estranged grandmother, Gwenyth, widow of Clint Wells, the mine foreman who was blamed for the disastrous silver mine collapse sixtysomething years ago. *Unfairly* blamed. That much she had discovered to be true.

Her progress had been slower than she would've liked, but she couldn't afford to give up now. Reuniting her family was the whole reason she'd come to Texas. Her mother wasn't even aware she was in Chatelaine. Morgana was being secretive to protect her mom because talking about the past was hard for her. At the age of eighteen her mom, Renee, moved to Tennessee and started a new life in a rural farming community where they made what little money they had by running a farm stand selling everything from fresh produce, honey and handmade goods. Renee had worked hard to build a life for them far away from her own mother's need for vengeance. Getting her hopes up for nothing was unacceptable.

They stopped beside his sporty luxury car. She wasn't even sure of the make or model. The lights flashed as he unlocked it with the key fob, and then he opened the door for her to get in.

"Thank you," she said and settled into the tan leather bucket seat that hugged her body like a lover. A shiver rippled all the way to her toes.

She shouldn't be thinking about lovers while she was already working so hard to resist her attraction to Bear Fortune. The oil baron who was way out of her league. In the time it took for him to round the hood of the car, she'd inhaled the scent of leather and admired the curving lines of the dashboard. A strip down the center around the controls was made from real wood, inlaid in a chevron pattern highlighted with a glossy coating.

For a tall guy, he easily slid into his seat in one swift and graceful movement, making her think of the prowling wildcats she loved watching at the zoo. And when he started the car, it purred and rumbled like said large powerful animal.

"This is a beautiful car. Have you had it long?"

"No. I just leased it when I got back from Brazil. I've always wanted an Aston Martin."

So that's what this is.

He seemed to be making his dreams come true, and that gave her hope that she could accomplish a few of her own by his age—which she thought was early thirties. "How did you get the nickname Bear?"

"I think it was because West couldn't say Barrington."

"That makes sense." Morgana couldn't seem to stop her nervous chatter. "I would love to go to Brazil someday. I hear there are some amazing waterfalls there."

"It's true. Iguaçú Falls is the largest broken waterfall in the world."

"Broken? Does that mean a lot of them side by side?" she asked.

"Exactly." His long fingers drummed on the leather steering wheel and a smile played on his lips, but his eyes remained on the road ahead. "It's made up of a chain of waterfalls. There are two hundred and seventy-five of them all fed by the Iguaçú River."

"I also like learning facts about the places I go,"

she murmured. "That must have been a wonderful vacation."

"It was for work. I was there for about three months. But I did slip away for a week to visit the falls."

"Didn't I hear that you're in the oil business?" she asked.

"I don't know. *Did* you hear that?" He cocked his head and shot her a brief glance.

She sighed inwardly. He was a tough one, just like Freya. "I must have, or it wouldn't have come to mind."

"Where'd you hear it?"

Apparently two could play the question game. She pretended to think about it, even though she knew exactly where she'd heard it. "I believe it was at Cowgirl Café when some of your cousins were sitting in the booth behind me." She fidgeted with her star charm to calm herself. She needed to keep her head about her and not get all dreamy-eyed. "Do you like the oil business?"

"Do you always ask so many questions?" It was said with a grin that lifted one corner of his mouth.

"I'm delightfully inquisitive. I know all kinds of interesting facts about Chatelaine."

"Well, now I guess we know how that happened."

"I'm just curious by nature. Always have been." It was true. Lots of people had told her that—some of them while rolling their eyes as they said it.

"I was consulting on a new offshore drilling project for a company who doesn't want to cut down rainforest to drill on land."

"That's admirable. How does one get a job like that?"

"I invented a new type of drill bit."

"Oh wow. An inventor. Impressive."

He shrugged like it was no big thing.

The ride was over too soon as he pulled up in front of Remi's Reads, and she opened her door. "Thanks for the lift."

"You're welcome. See you around, neighbor."

"If you need anything at all, you know where I am." Heat washed over her face, and she winced at the suggestive way that had sounded. "Like fresh towels or…" Her voice trailed off before she could embarrass herself further.

"Or toilet paper?" he quipped, using the exact words she'd been trying to avoid.

"Have fun with your brother." She practically leaped from the car, closing the door and then waving as he pulled away. Watching him drive away in his fancy car, she understood why he didn't need Freya to be his fairy godmother. Bear could grant his own wishes.

Chapter Three

Since the speed limit on this stretch of road was only twenty-five miles per hour, in between looking out his windshield, Bear watched Morgana growing smaller in his rearview mirror. She hadn't gone inside, just stood in front of the bookstore, watching him right back.

"What am I going to do with you, Morgana the Curious? Full of questions and so spirited." He hadn't stopped thinking about her since she'd danced on his bed, and he wanted her back on it. With him.

Bad idea, dude. Really bad idea.

There was no denying the instant spark between him and Morgana. Something so tempting and evocative. Like the finest dark chocolate and ultrasoft cashmere against bare skin. But falling into bed with the maid that lived a few doors down was reckless. Not because he thought she was beneath him. Never that. He'd started at the very bottom in life, literally abandoned in a park. It was because she wanted something from his family, and he knew all too well how initial sparks could burn down a life.

With a button on the leather steering wheel of his Aston Martin, he changed the radio to a country station and made the turn toward his brother's house. He loved the way this car handled, powerful yet smooth. Maybe he'd have to do more than just lease it.

He pulled up and parked in front of West's new house where he lived with his fiancée, Tabitha, and their one-year-old twin boys. Since he'd come to town, watching his brother with his adorable twin baby boys was making something paternal stir inside of him. He made his way up the front walk, which was lined with well-manicured grass, and stepped up onto the front porch to knock. There were a couple of comfy outdoor chairs and toys scattered about. Signs of the family life his brother was living.

Bear had come here to see for himself that West was alive and well, but he intended to keep his distance from anything involving his past, including his grandfather's widow, which was a challenge since she was staying at the same motel. He'd made a conscious decision to be about the here and now and to focus on the future. Always trying to outrun his past could get exhausting, but getting too close to anyone came with a big risk of losing them. It's why he liked to move from place to place because no one knew him well enough to know his tragic backstory.

The door opened, and Tabitha smiled at him. "Hi, Bear. Come on inside. West is just finishing up with a phone call and will be out of his office in a few minutes."

He kissed her cheek. "Good to see you again." He followed her from the front door to the living room where his nephews, Zach and Zane, were curled up together asleep on a blanket on the floor. It was the cutest thing he'd seen in a long time. He sat on the couch, and she took the chair across the room.

"Everyone is so glad you've come to Chatelaine. We're also glad to find out what you've been up to."

"Did you think it was something scandalous?" he asked dryly.

She chuckled and flipped her long blond hair over her shoulder. "We'd all been making guesses. A few I can remember were a spy, private detective and I believe someone guessed exotic dancer."

He laughed loud enough at that last one to wake up one of the babies. "Oops. Sorry about that."

"It's alright," she said and watched to see if the child would settle back down. "It's time for them to wake up from their nap."

The toddler sat up, rubbed his eyes and then smiled at him. Bear got down on the floor beside them. "Hey, there..." He tried to remember which twin this was.

"That's Zach," Tabitha filled in helpfully.

His nephew crawled his way, which happened to be across the top of his sleeping brother. The second twin was understandably a little crankier, and his mom went over to soothe him.

The little boy continued making his way over to Bear and crawled into his lap. "What's up, Zach man?"

The toddler babbled unintelligibly, and in no time,

both boys were bringing him toys and climbing on his body like a jungle gym. He'd only been around his nephews a few times, but they were sneaking into his very closed heart. At first it had surprised him, but after giving it a bit of thought, it also made him realize he was ready to be a dad.

The twins were giggling so hard at his silly faces that they were out of breath.

West came into the living room, and when Tabitha smiled at him, he crossed the room to give her a kiss. The love between them was obvious, and Bear really hoped they could make it last, even though he couldn't.

He no longer believed in forever love—catching his ex-wife with his best friend last year had knocked the fairy tale right out of him. Who can he trust if not a best friend and a wife? The answer? Himself. Only himself. He'd have to find a way to experience fatherhood without it including a wife. He could only count on his own actions and keeping his heart out of things was a must.

West sat down beside him and the boys. "Sorry about being on the phone when you got here."

"No worries. These two have kept me entertained."

The twins were excited to have two big guys to climb on now. However, when Zach and Zane began to get irritable and started squabbling with each other, their mother came into the room and scooped them up. "Time for you two rug rats to have dinner and a bath. Tell your Uncle Bear goodbye."

One babbled and one cried.

"Bye, boys. I'll see you again soon." He waved as their mom carried them away, one on each hip.

"Let's go out onto the porch and have a beer." West suggested.

"Sounds good."

Bear took a seat on the back porch while his brother grabbed the beers and thought about what he had observed over the last hour. West had come back from hiding after the criminal who threatened to hurt Tabitha had been killed and had the shock of a lifetime when he learned he was the father of twins. But he'd jumped in with both feet and become part of a real family. A *happy* family. His little brother was in love, and he prayed it was only the beginning of West's happily ever after. But most of all, he was grateful that his bro was alive.

West came out through the back door and handed Bear a long-necked amber bottle.

"Thanks." He studied his brother's face, noticing some of the lines of worry and stress had diminished.

"What? Why are you looking at me like I'm a science experiment?"

Bear shook his head and took a long pull on his drink, the ice-cold beer cooling his throat that had suddenly grown tight and burning from too much emotion coming at him all at once. "It's just really great to have you back from the dead, little brother."

"I can't tell you how good it is to be out of hiding. But if only I'd known…"

He knew what West was thinking without him saying it. If he'd only known Tabitha was pregnant.

West shook his head and rolled his shoulder in a new repetitive movement Bear had noticed since coming to town. He couldn't imagine what it would be like to have a bullet wound and was sorry his brother would have a permanent reminder of falling into the river after being shot and assumed dead.

"I missed so much." His voice was hoarse with tightly held pain.

Bear squeezed his uninjured shoulder. "But you haven't missed *everything*. And the boys are young enough that they won't remember a time when you weren't around."

"Good point." West took a long swallow of his beer.

"Tell me about the ranch where you were hiding out. How was it being a real cowboy?"

"The hard work at least kept me in shape, busy and exhausted enough not to go crazy. I can ride, rope, fix fence, brand cattle and a whole host of new skills."

"We sure are glad you're back with us," Bear said.

"Thanks, and we're all happy to see you, too. You know that it worries us when you're out of touch, but am I right to think you're living some of the adventure stories you told us when we were kids?"

Bear shot his brother a surprised look. "You remember those stories?"

"Of course. Your make-believe stories got us through a lot of tough nights."

They were quiet, remembering the nights their parents fought, saying more than three little boys needed to hear. When they would argue about who had an affair or who'd spent too much money, Bear would gather them all in one bed and tell them stories about the most exciting adventures he could think of. Exploring and discovering and fighting for good.

His adoptive parents, Peter and Dolly Fortune, hadn't been the best parents in the world, and even though there had been nights he and his two younger brothers had to fall asleep to the sounds of fighting and slamming doors, he had loved them and they him. He missed them since their fatal plane crash five years ago. He often wished he had a thicker skin because loss was hard for him.

"I think I'll start telling Zach and Zane those kinds of stories at bedtime," West told him. "Without adults yelling in the background."

"Good plan. It's never too early to start." Bear's thoughts once again went to his desire for a child of his own. A child that he could love and tell bedtime stories to each night. This time with stories that were based on his real-life adventures. A wish Freya could not grant. He'd have to figure this one out for himself. But how to do it without involving the big three: romance, his heart and hurting another person. That was the question.

Bear stretched out his legs and propped one snakeskin boot over the other. "Part of the reason I've stayed out of touch with everyone is because I thought I'd lost you forever. I know it seems opposite to pull away from family at a time when it's been proven you can lose them in an instant, but that's what I did."

"You always have been a lone wolf. But you know, you don't have to be alone forever."

Alone. Like he'd been as a toddler when his birth family abandoned him in a sandbox at the park. Alone now because his wife had tossed away their marriage. Maybe he was meant to be alone, but he didn't feel like having that discussion with West right now. "I know. I'm working on it. I've just been really busy."

"Are you dating anyone?"

An image flashed in his mind. Silky dark hair, mischievous green eyes and a lush smile. *Morgana.* Why was the pretty motel maid coming to mind? Anything happening with her was a bad idea, just like it was the last time he'd thought about it.

"No one lately. Guess I'm not eager to jump back into the fire and get burned again."

"I can understand that," his brother acknowledged. "Will you tell me what happened with your marriage?"

Bear's chest constricted as if wrapped with a metal band like it always did when he thought of his ex-wife and his ex-best friend. "The short version is, I came home early from a business trip to surprise her. Instead, I was the one who got the surprise. Not a good one."

West winced and took a sip of his beer. "Let me guess. She wasn't alone?"

"No, sir, she was definitely not alone." Acid burned in his stomach, and he rubbed his eyes, trying to ease the picture that had been burned into his brain. "She was naked and so was the man I thought was my best friend."

"Damn. That's rough. Sorry you had to go through that."

He ripped off a piece of the beer's paper label. "You're lucky to have the twins. I thought I'd have a kid by now, but it hasn't been in the cards for me." If he wanted to make something happen, he was going to have to do it himself.

"It's worth trying love again. You need to give it another chance, Bear. It's worth it."

"No thank you. It's a been-there-done-that-and-don't-plan-to-repeat-it kind of thing. I've been abandoned, lost parents, lost a brother—only for a while, thank God—and been cheated on by a wife and a friend. I think I'll stick to only temporary hookups." He didn't want to bring up the fact that he wanted an heir, because the problem was how to make that happen without entangling his heart with a woman.

"Are you going to the Fourth of July picnic at the park? We're taking the boys."

He was glad for the change of topic. "I didn't know about it, but sure. I'll meet you there."

Bear parked his car in the lot of the motel and saw Morgana struggling to get a piece of furniture up the stairs. She was lifting it up one stair at a time, then pausing to catch her breath before struggling to get it to the next one. He hurried over to her.

"Let me help you with that."

She looked startled to see him but then smiled. "That would be great."

It was a small dresser with the drawers removed. It was worn with a child's scribbles on one side and scars along the top. Something that should be going out of the motel and not being moved *into* it. "Does the owner often make you move furniture?"

She chuckled. "No. Someone set this out in front of their house for the heavy trash pickup, and I'm planning to refinish it and hopefully sell it."

He looked around them. "How did you get it from the house where you found it here to the motel?"

"I rolled it carefully down the road on my skateboard. But sadly, that doesn't work for the stairs."

"Wait, back up to the skateboard part."

"Someone gave it to me, but I can't do more than roll along on a flat surface. Do you skateboard?"

"Yes, but I haven't done it in years. Let me get this furniture for you." He stepped around her, picked up the dresser and went up the rest of the stairs. It weighed nothing compared to the equipment he regularly moved around on oil rigs. "Are we going to your room?"

"No. See where the drawers are stacked up beside that door? That's the storage room where I'll be working on it."

Once they got all of the pieces inside, she locked the door and then flapped her shirt to cool her body.

"Thanks for your help. Want a cold drink? I have some in my mini fridge."

He should say no. The two of them being alone in her room wasn't his smartest move, but he couldn't make himself decline. Consequences be damned. "That would be great."

When she flipped on the light in her motel room, he took in her space. There were splashes of color and touches that seemed fitting for the woman he was starting to know. A jewel-toned patchwork quilt on the bed, a purple scarf draped over her desk chair, a few belts on a doorknob and a painted table served as a kitchenette. Little terra-cotta pots of herbs were lined up along her windowsill and her book of Cinderella stories on her bedside table.

"Nice place you have here."

She looked at him with a slight tilt of her head as if trying to assess whether or not he was being serious.

"You did a good job of making it feel like a home with the plants and colors and stuff," he clarified.

What do I think I am? An interior decorator? I sound like a dumbass.

"Thanks." She got two Coca-Colas out of her tiny refrigerator and handed one to him.

He worked the flip-top on the ice-cold can of soda and it hissed as carbonated effervescence escaped, making his mouth water for the sweet, fizzy drink.

She rolled her cold can over her cheeks before opening it. "Mind if I ask you something?"

"Go for it."

"Why are you so against Freya's wish granting? Have all your dreams already come true?"

"The ones Freya could possibly grant have. I don't need her money. But I do have a wish I intend to grant on my own. I want an heir." Goosebumps popped up on Bear's skin. Why was he telling her this? He hadn't shared this with anyone. Barely even to himself.

She sat on the foot of her bed and ran the tip of one finger around the rim of her can. "You want to fall in love and marry and have a child?"

Just hearing the word *marriage* made his gut clench. "Love? No. Tried that. I don't believe in love."

Morgana's brow furrowed as if she felt bad for him. "I see."

"I only want an heir, but I'm stumped on how to do that without hurting another person."

"At least you aren't the kind of guy who goes around breaking hearts. But you do intend to love your child, don't you?"

He stiffened as his insides twisted. "Of course I'll love him or her. That's completely different."

He would never understand a parent not loving their own child and would never ever do what his birth family had done to him. He loved his adoptive family, but after his parents' death and then his whole marriage fiasco, losing people had become a sore point for him. That's why it had been so hard on him when they thought West was dead.

"Why don't you hire a surrogate?"

Morgana's voice pulled him from his spiraling

thoughts. "That sounds complicated," he answered gruffly.

Bear leaned his back against the wall beside her desk with a heavy sigh. In the years since he'd become rich, he wasn't used to being hindered from getting what he wanted, but this situation was tricky. If a child was involved, everything had to be considered very carefully.

Morgana kicked off her flip-flops, tucked her feet beneath her and flashed him a nervous smile. "If you tell me everything you know about Freya Fortune, maybe I can help you find a nice woman to have your baby. Or an agency that handles that kind of thing."

Something jolted inside him at the thought of *this* gorgeous, vibrant woman being the one to have his baby, but rather than let it show, he casually crossed one boot over the other. She was young and beautiful, and he got the feeling she was looking for the kind of happy endings found in one of her books. And he did not fit into that mold. "Why in the world do you want to know about Freya so badly?"

"I'm just curious. I've been cleaning her room for months, and she is kind of fascinating. Why is someone like her living in a place like this? She is so stylish and clearly has the money to rent a house or at least an apartment."

He'd recently thought the same thing. "I have money and I'm staying here."

"Are you planning to stay here for months on end?"

"Well, no." He followed her gaze to a stack of notebooks on her desk beside a couple of books about Chatelaine.

"Remember when I told you I was on a road trip when I came here?"

"Yes. You said you were stranded here when your car broke down."

"I've been traveling around the country collecting stories and doing research for a book I want to write about how a town's history makes it unique."

"A book? Like a novel or a nonfiction book?"

"You think I can't write? I did have some schooling back on the farm," she said with an exaggerated Southern accent.

He chuckled. "No. I didn't mean that at all. I'm just surprised. But intrigued. So, if you're traveling to collect stories, why have you stayed in Chatelaine for so long?"

"Because I ran out of money, and I've had to pause my trip to make some," she admitted. "And while I've been here the last few months, some stories have caught my attention."

"Meaning the mine disaster and the Fortune family. *My* family."

"Yes." She picked at a loose thread on her quilt. "Among other things."

"Well, you've come to the wrong person to ask about Freya. I don't know a thing about her." He studied Morgana for a moment, waiting for her to look at him. His phone rang in his pocket, and he pulled it out to see if it was important. It wasn't but it felt like the right time to make an exit. "I should get going so I can call them back. Thanks for the drink."

She stood and opened the door. "And thank you again for helping me with the dresser."

"Anytime. See you around, dancing queen." Morgana's door had barely closed, and Bear already wanted to see her again.

Chapter Four

Because there hadn't been many motel guests last night, work had been light today and Morgana was antsy and bored. She watered her little terra-cotta pots of herbs that were lined up on her windowsill and got herself a cold bottle of kombucha from her mini fridge. She so badly wanted to finally just come out with the truth of her identity—that she came to Chatelaine months ago to research her family history so that she could repair it. Until she got further along in her research, she had to keep the secret a while longer.

From under her bed, she pulled out the cardboard box of photos, letters and other information she'd collected while in Chatelaine. She'd started with limited information. She knew her grandmother Gwenyth's birthday was July 25 and had an old photo, but she hadn't been able to gather too much information because her mom, Renee, didn't like to talk about the grandparent Morgana had never met. She said it was to get away from Gwenyth's all-consuming desire for vengeance against the Fortune brothers for unfairly blaming her husband Clint Wells for the 1965 silver mine collapse and ruining the Wells name. What a wild family history she had.

Sighing, she sat on her bed and spread out the collection of clues. She didn't have the original notes left by a mystery person about there being a fifty-first miner, but she knew what they said. The first anonymous note had been found last fall behind Fortune Castle where the number fifty—memorializing the perished miners—was etched into the castle wall. A castle that was built by Wendell Fortune. The note said "There were fifty-one." A couple of months ago, another unsigned note had been tacked up on the community bulletin board in the park and said "Fifty-one died in the mine. Where are the records? What became of Gwenyth Wells?"

This note containing her grandmother's name was the one that was giving her the hope she needed to continue. There was someone else out there with the same questions she had. A couple of people had said their great-grandparents knew someone who died in the mine collapse, but no one had any real useful information.

Who was leaving these notes?

In her quest for answers, she'd been to the town archives at city hall and the ones at the *Chatelaine Daily News*, as well as the town's small history museum to read through old articles and study photos. From looking at old grainy photos of her grandmother that she'd found around town, the age range, and little things Freya had said and done, Morgana had started to wonder if Freya Fortune and her grandmother were one and the same, but that seemed so unlikely.

Freya is *Elias Fortune's widow.* Why would her grandmother ever marry the enemy who she blamed for killing her husband and ruining their family? It made no sense.

She spread out the faded photographs on the patchwork quilt that she'd helped her mom make years ago. She compared one she'd recently taken of Freya— without her knowledge—to a photo of her grandmother from the 1960s. But she just couldn't tell. Next, Morgana reread the stack of old letters Wendell's daughter, Ariella, had written to him, but once again nothing new or noteworthy jumped out at her.

Maybe it was time to make another trip to the museum. She slipped on her tennis shoes and started her walk. Bear's car wasn't in the parking lot. Too bad the prince of bachelors wasn't around to give her a ride in style.

The Chatelaine Museum was a modest old historical museum in a white adobe house with a red tile roof. It had aged wooden floors and photos hung gallery style on every wall, and the hallway had an enormous hand-drawn map of the town with street names written in a neat but faded cursive.

She hoped that after her recent research, something she saw would spark an idea, or she might notice something she hadn't before. The old flooring creaked as she stepped inside and closed the heavy wooden door. After saying hello to the young woman sitting at the front desk, she walked slowly along each wall, studying every photo and reading every description, but no matter how hard she looked, she had no more information than she'd started the day with.

Another waste of time.

Feeling a bit discouraged about all the dead ends and unanswered questions, Morgana came out of the Chatelaine Museum and shielded her eyes from the afternoon sun. Digging into her purse, she put on her pair of cheap sunglasses for the trek back to the motel. And all the while she kept an eye out for Bear or his Aston Martin, but there was no sign of her crush.

The next afternoon, Morgana was walking to the town's Fourth of July celebration at the park and once again wishing she had the money to get her car repaired so she wouldn't have to depend on her own two feet all of the time.

"I'm the one who needs a fairy godmother," she mumbled.

A car pulled to a stop at the curb beside her. The automatic window rolled down and Wendell smiled at her. "Can I give you a ride somewhere, young lady?"

A fairy godfather worked, too. "I'm headed to the park for the Fourth of July celebration."

"I'm going that way. Hop in."

"Thanks." She climbed in and clicked her seat belt in place. She really wanted to ask Wendell about the missing letter he was supposed to be looking for, but she wasn't sure if she should jump right to it. "Are you joining the celebration today?"

He turned down the country music playing on the radio. "For a little while. I'm meeting some of the grandkids."

"Oh, good. How have you been feeling lately? I know your hip gives you trouble."

"I guess I'm about as okay as an old man my age can feel. Make sure to have fun while you're young."

"I'm working on it. Have you found the missing letter from your daughter, Ariella?"

"No, but I'll keep looking for it."

Morgana kept her sigh of frustration on the inside. She really needed to catch a break.

Bear had never been to the city park but found it easily. If he could navigate around the world, he could manage a small Texas town. The Chatelaine Fourth of July celebration was being held here, and he'd promised to meet his brothers. The park had beautiful trees, a walking path, a play structure and a covered pavilion with a concrete floor. There was a community bulletin board near the pavilion. Bear had been told this is where one of the mysterious notes about a fifty-first miner had been posted.

The park was decorated with red, white and blue streamers, balloons and flags. Food trucks were lined up in one area with a tempting variety of food, sweets and icy cold beverages. The event was noisy and crowded but he spotted West and Camden in line for drinks. West had a cowboy hat on over his dark blond hair and his youngest brother had on a baseball cap.

Bear slipped up behind them and grabbed each of them by the shoulder like he'd done when they were kids and caught them doing something mischievous. "What kind of trouble are you two getting into?"

West slugged him in the arm. "Hey, brother Bear. Nothing yet. Other than getting caught giving the twins candy this morning."

"Glad you made it out to meet up with us today," Camden added.

"Me, too." He meant it. He was really glad to see his brothers. "I've had a lot of work that's kept me on my computer. Closing one deal and working on a couple of others."

Camden moved forward in the line. "Good to hear your business is doing well. You should be proud of your accomplishments."

"Really proud," West said. "Tabitha and my boys will be here any minute and might want a place to sit. Y'all go grab one of those tables before they're taken, and I'll wait here for the drinks."

"Where is your girlfriend?" Bear asked Camden as they wove through people to get to an empty table.

"Haley was here earlier but had a few things to do. She's meeting us later for dinner at Cowgirl Café. You're still going, right?"

"I'll be there," he assured his brother.

"How is it living in the motel?"

"It's fine. Clean and comfortable, but I sure do miss room service."

"The pretty, inquisitive maid can't help you out with your needs?"

Even though he knew the comment was said in good fun and only teasing, Bear's hackles rose, and he gave Camden a hard stare.

His youngest brother raised his hands. "Whoa. I know that look on your face. You're protective of her."

"No, I'm not." The lie rolled right off his tongue to land like a lead ball on his big toe.

"You know I'm just kidding around. I didn't mean anything by that comment."

"I know."

West joined them at the table with three iced teas. "No sign of Tabitha and the twins?"

Camden took one of the drinks. "Not yet."

"I want a child." The words left Bear's mouth in a rush and earned him blank stares from both brothers.

"Like adopting one?" Camden asked.

"No. Adoption worked out great for me and lots of other people, but I'm talking about a child who is biologically mine. I don't have any blood relations. Well, I do somewhere, but I don't know any of them."

"You know the blood running through your veins doesn't matter to us, right?" Camden said gruffly.

"Yes, I do"

"But I understand what you're saying." West crunched a piece of ice between his back teeth. "Looking into the identical faces of my boys, it's an amazing feeling you can't describe."

Now they were just getting too emotional, and he needed to rein it in. "I also need an heir," Bear blurted out and got raised eyebrows from both men.

"You need one for your massive fortune?" Camden asked with a chuckle.

They clearly didn't realize how much money he'd earned off the patents for drilling equipment and oil wells. "Let me rephrase that. I *want* an heir. But how to get a baby is the challenge. How can I have a baby without involving romance, love or hurting a woman?"

His brothers looked at one another and then burst out laughing. "Dude, good luck with that," West said. "There's no way to escape any of the three, let alone one."

That answer wasn't reassuring in the least. They paused the conversation when Tabitha headed their way with the boys in a double stroller.

He chatted with his family, held his nephews and ate a hotdog. A little while later, Bear caught sight of Morgana across the park. She was dressed in denim shorts, a flowy white top with red flowers embroidered around the neck and sleeves, and she had a white daisy stuck in her ponytail. "I'm going to go say hello to someone."

West followed his line of sight. "Bro, do you know what you're doing? She's the one asking all the questions."

"True, but she wants to know about Freya as much as I do. I want to find out what she knows. Questions can go both ways."

"Just be careful," his brother said.

"Will do." Bear slipped away from the group and made his way over to where Morgana was examining things at a craft booth. "You look like you could use a snow cone."

She turned to him with a smile. "I think you're right."

They began walking side by side as if it was a completely normal thing for them to do. His hand tingled with a desire to reach out and take hold of hers, so he hooked his thumbs in the pockets of his jeans. Maybe West was right to tell him to be careful, because he realized that he did feel a connection and a sort of protectiveness for her. But *why*?

"Are you staying for the fireworks?" she asked.

"I hadn't really planned on it."

"Hal said there's a good view of them from the motel."

"That's handy. We can just step outside of our doors later and watch the show." That had sounded like an invitation, and he knew he shouldn't have said it, but he wasn't sorry. "But you're probably planning to watch from here."

"No. I'll be back at the motel. I don't think I can take being in a big crowd from now until after dark."

"A woman after my own heart. I'm not a fan of crowds either." They stopped in front of the food truck that served snow cones. "What's your favorite flavor?"

"Blue coconut. But I always end up with a blue tongue. If I'd choose watermelon, which I also like, at least my tongue would be red." Her hands moved animatedly as she talked.

He couldn't resist smiling at her excited chatter. They reached their turn at the window, and he ordered both of the flavors she'd mentioned and then held them toward her. "Take your pick."

She tapped her chin with her index finger. "I think I should taste each before I make my decision. Unless you're afraid of my girl cooties."

He laughed loud enough that a few people looked in his direction. "Nope. No fear here."

"Good." She took the watermelon snow cone and pressed her mouth to the soft, snow-packed ice, and then made a soft moaning sound of pleasure. "Mmm. Cold and sweet. That really hits the spot."

His brain went straight to places that it shouldn't. Like the "spot" on her neck where a star charm rested against her skin that was rosy from the warmth of the day. Instead, he tasted the blue snow cone.

They started walking again in no particular direction. "Is it a really long flight from here to Brazil?" she asked.

"Pretty long. About nine or ten hours. I usually travel at night and try to sleep." Having a private plane helped make any trip a lot more comfortable.

"Where are you off to next?"

"I'm not sure yet. It depends on a few deals I have working." He held out the blue snow cone and they traded without having to say anything. Something about taking a bite of the watermelon snow cone where her mouth had been made him feel like a teenager who had a crush.

"It sounds to me like you don't like to stay in one place for long."

"That's true." He was a jet-setter, never settling in any place for too long. "Aren't you a bit of a traveler yourself? You mentioned being on a road trip."

"I'm only just getting started with my adventures. I've barely been anywhere, yet."

He found himself getting excited that she craved adventures just like he did. He had ever since he could remember, and now he was living them, but factoring in a woman he'd just met as part of any adventure was exactly what he should *not* be doing. "You were right about something. Your tongue is blue." He chuckled when she stuck it out to check.

"Let me see yours," she said and then grinned. "Yours is, too. Well, actually it's turning purple from the mix of red and blue."

At Morgana's request, they stopped at a booth for the animal shelter. Some of the hopeful pets were in kennels and a round pen had been set up in the center so people could get a good look at the excited puppies.

She dropped to her knees in the grass beside the pen. "I miss having an animal around."

"I guess they don't allow pets at the motel?"

"Freya has a cat."

"She does?" He knelt to rub the soft belly of a chocolate-brown puppy who licked his hand and wagged his tail so hard that his whole back end wiggled from side to side.

"Have you seen the orange cat running around the motel?"

"Yes. I thought it was a stray."

"He was, but now his name is Sunset. He attached himself to Freya, and since she is a semipermanent guest, Hal had no problem with it."

If animals liked Freya and she liked them, she couldn't be all bad. At least that's what he'd found to be true over the years.

"Aww, this one is adorable." She held up a puppy with sleek black fur and let him lick the tip of her nose.

"You shouldn't say that so loud," he whispered. "The others will get jealous."

"Never fear. I have plenty of good words to describe all of them. There's precious and darling and cutie-pie."

She continued naming the pups, but he was too busy focusing on the way her lips moved as she talked.

They stayed there long enough to pet all the cute animals who were looking for a permanent home. As much as he wanted a pet, he didn't have a home to take one to. He rented places that were conveniently located for whatever he was doing at the time. His skin prickled.

If I don't have a home for a pet, how do I expect to make a home for a child?

Whatever it took, he would figure it out. He had the money to make it happen.

Morgana touched his arm. "Bear? Are you okay?"

"Absolutely." He looked at his watch, hiding his face long enough to get his expression under control. "I'm supposed to meet up with my family."

"I appreciate you hanging out with me for a while," she said softly.

"It was my pleasure." He meant it. The words weren't just an idle pleasantry like they would be with some people. He truly enjoyed this woman's company. But all too soon, his time with her was up.

As much as he wanted to ask her to come to dinner with him, he couldn't. His family was cautiously wary about Morgana, with different members having different opinions about her. He knew she was sweet and could sing and liked to dance. She was funny and enticingly beautiful in her eclectic style, but he didn't know enough about her to bring her to a meal with his family. Just happening to meet up as a group would be one thing, but him purposely bringing her would look too much like they were more than casual acquaintances.

"Thanks for indulging me with two flavors of snow cones. Have fun with your family. I guess I'll see you around the motel."

Was that a flash of disappointment he saw on her face? He was feeling a bit of that himself. "Yes, you will."

At the Cowgirl Café, owned by his cousin Bea Fortune, his family had a big table in a back corner. Of course, the news about him slipping away to talk to Morgana had made the rounds. Some of them were curious if she was after his money and warned him that he'd have to look out for that kind of thing now that he was wealthy. But they didn't all feel that way. Haley thought Morgana was nice and didn't mean any harm to anyone. Bear was starting to believe the same thing, but he hadn't gotten as far as he had in business by jumping to conclusions too quickly. Caution and plenty of consideration was always a must.

Bear ate too much, but everything at his cousin's restaurant was so good. He ended up with ketchup on his shirt courtesy of one of his nephews and chocolate sauce from the other twin. He laughed a lot, which felt really good, but he made sure to leave in time to get back to the motel before the fireworks. Resisting the draw of watching them with Morgana was too much and he gave up fighting it because he just couldn't think of a good enough reason at the moment.

Bear left Cowgirl Café just before dark, and the sun was setting as he pulled into the motel. He found himself automatically looking around for Morgana, but she wasn't outside. Hopefully, she'd come out soon to watch the fireworks, but if she didn't, should he knock on her door? He parked his car and picked up a book that had fallen onto the floorboard before heading toward his room.

"Barrington, do you have a minute to talk, please?"

Bear stopped and turned to face Freya Fortune. He'd been dodging her but had been too busy thinking about the lovely maid to pay enough attention to his surroundings. It was unusual for him to be so unaware. Another reason not to let himself get too deeply involved with Morgana or any other woman. But he might as well get this talk with dear old stepgranny over with, because he had some questions of his own. He glanced at his watch to suggest he had somewhere to be.

"Sure. I have a few minutes."

Her tense expression turned into a tentative smile. "Let's go sit over here."

He followed her to an outdoor seating area not far from her door. They sat in retro metal chairs that looked like they were from the 1950s and had been repainted many times. Currently, they were a bright cherry red.

Freya sat with a straight spine and folded her hands in her lap. As Morgana had mentioned the other day, she wore designer clothes and expensive jewelry and could clearly afford to live somewhere grand, yet she was living in an old motor lodge. He was only here temporarily to see his family and finish a business deal, but Freya seemed to be staying for the long haul.

He couldn't understand why she hadn't rented or even bought a house in town.

"As I'm sure you've been told, I'm here to honor your grandfather's last will and testament," she said.

"Yes. I've heard the stories. My family has given me the rundown."

"You're the last grandchild on my list, and I'd really like to help you. Will you please tell me your most fervent wish?"

"That's private, sorry," he answered brusquely. "And it's not anything you can help me with."

She sighed and fidgeted with a large diamond ring. "There must be *something...*"

"I already have more money than I know what to do with. I don't need any of Elias's."

"Maybe I can help you with something money can't buy then. Just think about it."

The old woman seemed so sad and tired. He suddenly felt for her and didn't want to add to her distress by being rude. Maybe she really had loved Elias Fortune that much and her mission was meant to honor her deceased husband. But the whole thing was all so strange. "I promise I'll think about it. Have a nice night, Freya."

"You, too, Bear."

He walked briskly toward the stairs to the second-floor walkway before she changed her mind and wanted to talk about something else. Bear had come here to see West and other family members. Not to get mixed up in old family drama and the wishes of a deceased grandfather he'd never known. He was about the here and now and the future. A future he would be in charge of. Wishing couldn't help him get what he wanted most. He'd have to do that for himself. Luckily, he had more than enough money to take care of and protect a child.

Once he was in his room, he took off the food-stained shirt he'd worn all day, washed his hands and face, brushed his teeth and put on a clean T-shirt. He was ready for some fireworks...of one kind or another. And he could think of a couple of good options. Discovering the taste of Morgana Mills's lips was currently top of the list.

Chapter Five

After a day at the town's Fourth of July celebration in the park, Morgana took a refreshingly cool shower and changed into a red dress that showed off more cleavage than usual, but she'd found it at the second-hand store and couldn't resist. The cotton fabric fell in soft folds from the empire waist to right above her knees. It made her feel feminine and desirable.

Would this dress make Bear think she was trying to seduce him? She gazed at her reflection in the mirror on the medicine cabinet above the pink bathroom sink. She wasn't completely inexperienced, but she had no doubt that he had plenty of practice with women and was probably used to them dressing way sexier than this.

"You don't even know if you'll see him again tonight," she said to herself. But having hope was never a bad thing.

She brushed her hair once more and put on mint lip gloss. In preparation for what, she didn't know. Bear was likely still with his family somewhere celebrating the nation's birthday. Not to mention, she shouldn't be doing anything to encourage Barrington Fortune. The wealthy oil baron who wanted someone to have a baby for him. Not with him, but for him. Emphasis on the *for*. He wasn't a good dating option. Not good at all.

"So, what is it that you think you're doing then?" her rebellious reflection asked with a big grin like a lovestruck teenager. She rolled her eyes at herself and went to find her shoes.

When she turned down the music playing on her phone, the screensaver appeared. It was her favorite picture of her and her mom when she'd been about ten. They didn't look much alike, but they were best friends. Even so, she envied Bear and all the Fortunes their large extended family. She remembered wonderful celebrations back on the farm. Everyone there was *like* family, but when it came right down to it, it was only her and her mom.

The fireworks would start soon, so she slipped on her flip-flops to go outside. If Bear wasn't back at the motel, maybe Freya would like to watch the fireworks with her. It would be another chance to get to know the mysterious older woman. But when she opened her door, the rush of sensations in her belly were like the flash of Fourth of July sparklers.

"Hello, neighbor." Bear had his folded arms propped on top of the railing.

"Hey, there." He was wearing a plain white T-shirt that was bright against his olive complexion and was just tight enough to show off sculpted muscles without looking like he was trying too hard. A tease, which she'd discovered was very onbrand for him. "I wasn't sure if you were still with your family or not."

"I got back a few minutes ago."

The night sky lit up followed closely by a boom and shower of sparkly crackles. It was followed closely by another, the boom's vibration traveling through her body and making her shiver. The breeze carried the faintest hint of black powder and the spicy scent of Bear's cologne.

"Looks like you got out here just in time," he said.

"Want to sit on the stairs? They're facing the perfect direction to see the show."

"Lead the way."

She sat first, and he lowered to sit beside her on the top step. The colorful display went on in front of them, but she was more aware of his body so close to hers. The heat of him. The sizzle of energy. If she wasn't careful, she'd catch fire and be about as subtle as one of those cone-shaped fireworks that jetted a fountain of shimmery sparkles.

"Did you say something?" he asked.

Oh, Lord, what did I say?

She had a troublesome habit of expressing some of her thoughts aloud, and since she was frequently alone, it usually didn't matter. But right now, it mattered. "I was just exclaiming over the fireworks. They're so beautiful."

"Very beautiful." He was smiling at her when he said it in a low, seductive voice.

A shower of tingles danced over her skin, leaving her momentarily weightless. "Who taught you to flirt?"

He laughed, a deep and very pleasant sound. "I guess it just comes naturally. Do you want me to stop?"

"Let's not get crazy now. I wouldn't want you to go against your nature."

With his arm brushing against hers, he met her gaze full on. "You are a most unique woman, Morgana Mills."

Her throat tightened at the sound of a last name that wasn't hers. Being deceptive did not come easily, and she prayed her face wasn't colored with guilt. "I'm trying to decide if unique is a good thing."

"I like unique things, so yes, it's good." Another firework exploded and sparks reflected in his brown eyes like a galaxy of stars. "You're refreshingly real."

"I try to be."

"You're also really young," he remarked.

"Not that young. I'm closer to thirty than twenty."

Bear quirked a brow. "By how much?"

"Well…a few months."

That made him chuckle. "I've got seven years on you."

"Women mature faster. So, twenty-five and thirty-two are practically the same age." She was enjoying their quick back and forth banter. At first, he'd made her nervous, but she'd discovered he was easy to talk to.

At the same moment, they turned to one another to comment on a particularly spectacular firework, and her breath caught. They were so close she could almost feel the heat of his mouth, burning for their first kiss.

A door slammed behind them, and they sprang apart. A teenage girl, who was obviously mad, stormed across the walkway, and they had to stand to let her get down the stairs.

The spell was broken. Disappointing but likely for the best. Morgana reminded herself that she had no experience with men like him. Cinderella's magical night only lasted a short time, and it would be the same with the world-traveling Bear Fortune. Living happily ever after with a prince in a castle was only in fairy tales and movies.

Although...there was a castle in town, and it just so happened that Fortune Castle belonged to someone in Bear's family.

The next day, Bear went out to his cousin Asa Fortune's dude ranch for a family barbecue. The weather was as perfect as you could get for a summer day. It was still hot, but the sky was filled with thick clouds that blocked out some of the sun's most oppressive heat, and a steady breeze kept the air moving. It carried the mouthwatering scent of food on the grill and the earthy scent of plants. They were celebrating a combination of a birthday, an anniversary and something else he'd forgotten. He had five new cousins who no one had known about until recently. They were Wendell Fortune's grandchildren, and he was still working on getting all their names straight.

He moved off to the outer edge of the group and stood in the shade of an oak tree while his siblings, cousins, and their families and significant others broke into groups to talk and laugh. Kids and toddlers were running around, and babies were crawling and crying. And Bear was hanging back taking it all in. He was fine with his own company, but being around so much family was making him want to spend more time with them than he'd planned.

As long as he could retreat to his own space now and then to recharge. But watching them interact was also making him want something more for himself. One couple, whose names he thought were Cooper and Alana, kissed and smiled at one another, and his mind flashed to Morgana. He cursed under his breath and took a long pull on his bottle of beer.

He did not want a serious relationship and absolutely not another marriage. That deal was off the table. All he wanted was a child of his own. And the occasional no-strings-attached company of a woman. Maybe a friends-with-benefits arrangement.

He enjoyed Morgana's company, but last night it had taken all of his willpower not to kiss her as they sat side by side on the stairs watching fireworks. And he'd almost given in to his desire when he caught the scent of mint from her glossy mouth and swayed in her direction, only to be interrupted by a pouting teenager.

He had a strong feeling Morgana would be a fire-cracker in bed, but the level of emotional attraction to her fun-loving nature could make it harder to keep his heart out of it. He wasn't sure if he could safely have a friends-with-benefits thing with her. She was young and struck him as a passionate woman who would likely want more than he had to give. He'd married a passionate woman, and that hadn't gone well at all.

His cousin Bea's fiancé, Devin Street, walked his way. He was the owner of the *Chatelaine Daily News*, and they'd only talked briefly, but he liked the man.

"I think you have the right idea hanging out over here," Devin said.

"Best way to take it all in. I'm also trying to figure out who belongs to who."

Devin laughed. "That might take a while. But I'm happy to help you out where I can."

"Do you know Morgana Mills? She's a maid at the motel."

"Yes. I know her. Morgana has been to my newspaper's archives a few times."

Bear swatted at a bee buzzing around his drink. "I know she's been asking a lot of questions about the Fortune family."

"She's also been asking about the 1965 silver mine collapse."

"She told me she loves history and wants to write a book. Do you think that's true or is she after something else?"

"Well, she goes through old town photos and really does read old articles and takes a lot of notes, so it's not out of the question." Scrubbing a hand over his jaw,

Devin mused, "And being a newspaper man, I'm used to reporters who ask plenty of questions. So I guess it doesn't seem that odd to me."

That eased Bear's mind about her...somewhat. Before they could talk more about it, two little redheaded boys wearing blue superhero capes ran right between them, the smaller one chasing the bigger one with a foam sword.

"That's Jacob and Benjy. Your cousin Damon's kids."

Bear chuckled when the older one performed a very dramatic death scene that involved rolling around on the grass with a variety of accompanying noises. They certainly had a lot of energy. Another reason to have a kid sooner rather than later was doing it before he was too old to play with and chase after them. Which was admittedly many years from now, but he also wanted to be able to keep up with grandchildren as well.

The next morning, Bear closed his laptop after a frustrating but successful business meeting with people from three countries. He needed to rework a proposal, but right now, he was too distracted and couldn't give it his full attention.

He couldn't get Morgana out of his mind. The wheels of her cleaning cart clunked across the walkway outside of his room, and like a teenager who had no control over himself, he opened his door. "Good morning."

"Hi, Bear."

Her sweet smile made something warm swirl about in his chest.

"Is now a good time to clean your room? If not, I can come back later."

"It's perfect timing. I just finished a virtual meeting."

She was biting her cheek in an obvious attempt not to laugh. "Is that why you're wearing a dress shirt and tie with jogging shorts and no shoes?"

He glanced down at himself and laughed. "Yes, ma'am. That would be the reason."

"I don't blame you a bit. I would do the same thing."

He stepped back into his room and helped her pull the cart over the threshold, making a mental note to buy new ones for the motel. She and the other maid deserved to work with good equipment that didn't frustrate them.

He loosened his tie and pulled it off then started unbuttoning his shirt. He didn't have on an undershirt like he normally would, and he couldn't deny enjoying the flicker of interest he caught as she tried not to look at him standing there in nothing but a pair of shorts.

"I should probably start with the bathtub." Her gaze once again landed on him before she disappeared into the bathroom.

As she worked out of sight, he put on a supersoft Dolce & Gabbana T-shirt, a luxury he could now afford. He sat at his computer, scrolled through a couple of websites and ordered several of the best carts he could find. He had them shipped anonymously to the Chatelaine Motel and wondered if they would figure out that he was the one who'd done it.

All too soon, Morgana had finished cleaning his room and moved on, and he was bored. He called Camden and then West, but both of his brothers were busy and couldn't hang out. The baby twins giggling in the background had tugged at his heart and caused a flash of jealousy, which made him once again think he was doing the right thing by deciding to become a father.

Although he usually liked being alone with his thoughts, right now they kept returning to the dangerous idea of Morgana being the one to have a baby for him. It would make things so simple if she would agree to be his surrogate.

If she was the woman that he thought she was, Morgana was just who he'd been looking for in a mother for his baby. Why? It was simple. Her cheery personality and being funny without even trying. Her go-get-'em attitude when she did things like haul old furniture upstairs because she wanted to make something old new again. And yes, her beauty certainly didn't hurt matters. There could be attraction and fun between them, but allowing romantic love to get mixed up in things was a terrible idea.

He didn't want his child to have parents who fought because there was hurt and jealousy. Keeping romantic expressions of love out of the equation was the only way to assure that.

Morgana might be young, at only twenty-five, but she was down-to-earth and knew how to take care of herself. She called it the way she saw it. If she agreed to do it, he wouldn't have to go through a long drawn-out search for a surrogate. Having her agree would make things so easy.

And fun.

He couldn't believe he was seriously considering asking her to be the mother of his child, but it would be mutually beneficial. She was a maid living in one room of a small motor lodge, and he knew she could use the money. While talking to the motel owner, Hal, he'd discovered why she walked everywhere. Her car had broken down and needed a lot of repairs that she was saving up for.

Bear stopped pacing and snapped his fingers. "I'll get her car repaired or just buy her a new one."

He shook his head, dismissing the idea of a new car. That was too much like a bribe. He would just repair the one she already had. Much easier to write that off as just one friend helping out another, and it would be a start to showing her how her life could be made so much easier. He could pay her a fortune to have his child and she'd never have to scrub a toilet or a bathtub for a stranger again.

That's it. His mind was made up.

I'm going to ask Morgana to have my baby.

Chapter Six

Morgana was about to make a sandwich when someone knocked on her door.

Please, let it be Bear.

The thought came in a flash, startling her with its intensity. Like one of the ladies on the farm in Tennessee used to say, this needed to be nipped in the bud right quick. She absolutely could not fall in love with Bear.

She looked through the peephole and her spirits lifted along with a giddy nervousness that made her pulse trip over itself.

Wish granted.

She checked her reflection in the mirror above the small dresser and then opened the door. "Hello, neighbor. Do you need to borrow a cup of flour?"

He smiled big enough to show perfect white teeth. "I wouldn't mind some sugar."

Was he hinting at something...like a kiss? "I actually do have sugar."

"What I'd really like to do is talk to you about something."

"Sure. Come on in." She stepped aside and swept

out her arm as if ushering him into an exclusive event. "What's on your mind?"

Bear crossed the room, lowered halfway as if he'd sit on the foot of her bed, but then he straightened and started pacing. "I have an offer to discuss."

"Like a business deal?" She hadn't seen him like this. He was jumpy and unsure, and it was starting to make her nervous.

"Kind of." He paused and faced her. "First let me say, I don't think you're a woman motivated by money. I happen to have more experience than I'd like with people who are."

Where was he going with this odd topic of conversation? "I appreciate your assessment of me, but I'm not sure why you're bringing that up. Do you need an assistant or extra maid services or something along those lines?"

"No. Nothing like that. Well, I guess it would fall in the something else category. What would you think about a million dollars to have a baby for me?"

She laughed and waited for him to do the same and then get to the real reason for his visit. But he didn't laugh. He didn't even smile. "Wait. Are you being serious?"

"Yes, I am. Completely serious." He stood tall with his feet braced slightly apart. His body language now screaming *confident businessman*.

Suddenly dizzy, she sidestepped to her bed and sat down hard. "You want me to have a baby for you?"

"That's the idea."

Could he actually be serious? "And how do you see me fitting into my own baby's life?"

"I haven't thought that far ahead." He pulled out the wooden chair from her tiny desk, straddled it in the wrong direction and propped his arms on the back.

"I see, so you envision what? That I have this baby for you, hand him or her over, take my million and walk away?"

He grimaced and pinched the bridge of his nose that had a slight crook from being broken. "It sounds bad when you put it like that. I can assure you that I am in fact a human with real feelings and emotions."

Morgana wasn't so sure about that at the moment. How could he possibly expect her to go along with such a wacky idea? "I think you need to take some time and come back when you have a well-thought-out plan." Not that she intended to have his child, she just wanted to make him *think* about what he was doing. The enormity of the favor he was asking of her.

"You make a good point."

"I bet you're more prepared than this when you make big oil deals."

"You're right." He rubbed a hand through his thick, dark hair, and his exhalation was long and slow as if to calm himself. "I got excited about the idea and jumped the gun. Can we talk more about it over dinner tonight?"

A quiver swept through her. She might be unwilling to have his child for money, but dinner seemed so mild in comparison. It was too good to pass up.

Why am I so drawn to this man?

It really wasn't hard to figure out. He was charismatic in a way that drew her in and made her want to see what he'd do next, and he was so handsome that looking at him was a treat for the eyes, but his guarded heart made her own ache. Maybe she could help redirect his misguided notions. "Dinner sounds nice. Where are we going and what's the dress code? I only have one nice dress with me."

His smile eased into the one she saw most often. Playful and a little bit devilish. "You should wear your dress. I like down-home restaurants like my cousin Bea's Cowgirl Café, but tonight, we'll be fine dining at the LC Club."

The words *fine dining* made her pulse pick up speed. "I've never been there."

"You'll like it." He looked at the digital clock on her bedside table. "Can I pick you up in an hour and a half?"

"That works for me," she said, trying not to let her eagerness show too much.

Once she closed her door behind Bear, she leaned her back against it and covered her face. "What just happened?" She did a little happy dance.

She'd already taken a shower, so she curled her hair into loose waves and did her makeup a bit more dramatically than her normal two coats of mascara and a touch of neutral eye shadow. For a date at a fancy restaurant, she added darker shadow, eyeliner, blush and lipstick. The blush was probably unnecessary because her cheeks would be rosy just from being with a man she found so attractive. A man who was so wrong for her. She wanted love and marriage and children she would raise as a partner with her husband. Apparently, Bear had no desire to fit into that lifestyle.

"Plus, he doesn't even live here, and he'll be jetting off to who knows where before I know it."

Which meant that anything that happened between them would only be a fling, not a relationship, and certainly not her being his baby mama. Did she want to have a fling with Bear?

The raucous butterfly dance going on in her stomach gave her the answer. Yes. Yes, she did.

But *did* and *should* were two entirely different things. She'd never done such a thing. All of her romances had been committed relationships, but maybe this was something everyone needed to do at least once in their life. Have a brief, passionate love affair you could look back on and know you didn't miss out on anything.

"I'll see how things go tonight at dinner, and then I'll make a decision."

She didn't have to decide at this very moment. She pulled her one nice dress from the postage stamp-sized closet, held it out in front of her and sighed. It was a black dress without much flair. The fabric was silky with a fitted bodice, a scalloped off-the-shoulder neckline and a full skirt. She put it on and added a thin silver chain belt that matched the adornment on her pair of nice black sandals and simple silver hoop earrings. Then she put her ID, lipstick, some cash and her phone into the emerald velvet clutch she'd made from a fabric remnant leftover from when they made curtains to glam up their small cottage living room.

Morgana was finally ready, but she still had some time to kill before Bear would be here to pick her up. For their *date*. She squealed and spun to make her skirt flair out around her, just like her excitement. She really needed to chill and act her age. She was twenty-five. Not fifteen.

She'd FaceTime with her mom. That would calm her down, even though Morgana felt guilty about deceiving her mother about where she was living. But if Renee Wells knew her daughter was in Chatelaine— the town she said she'd never return to—or that she was searching for her grandmother, she would be unhappy. Morgana didn't want to upset her mom about anything until she established a connection with her grandmother.

She had hoped to be able to tell her mom she'd found Gwenyth Wells or at least have something to report long before now, but she still hadn't found enough clues.

I need to be a better detective.

She had the sudden urge to watch an old episode of *Murder, She Wrote*. Jessica Fletcher would know what to do, and probably would've had this thing figured out by now. Since they'd only gotten a few TV channels on the farm while she was growing up, she'd rewatched the complete series on DVD many times over.

You'd think she would've learned a few tips and tricks for solving a mystery. At least she wasn't dealing with murder. Or *was* she? The silver mine collapse did have some suspicious circumstances surrounding it.

Morgana grabbed her phone and made the call. After a few rings, her mom answered. Her curly hair was pulled back with a leather headband, and her cheeks were pink from a day spent outdoors, probably in the orchard.

"Hi, honey. I was just thinking of you."

"What were you doing that made you think of me?"

"Looking at your baby picture on the mantel." Renee turned the phone to show her, as if she hadn't known it was there her whole entire life.

"Do you need me to take a selfie and send you a new photo?"

"Yes, please. I miss you. But I'm glad you're having a grand adventure." Her mom got comfy on their couch that was draped with several quilts that covered the worn spots. "You look so pretty tonight. Do you have a party...or a date?" she said with a wide grin that showed her dimples.

"Actually, I do have a date."

"Oh goodie, tell me everything about him. And start at the beginning..."

Morgana smiled and felt her tension begin to ease. There was no way she was going to tell her everything, but she was excited to share some of the details about Bear. Her mom was going to love the story about sharing snow cones.

* * *

Bear started to pull on a suit coat, but decided it was too hot for that level of dress. Gray slacks and a pale pink Prada dress shirt would have to do. After a quick check in the mirror to make sure he hadn't missed a bit of shaving cream, he brushed his hair. It was getting long on top, and it was time for a trim, but he had no idea where to go for one in Chatelaine. In the oil fields he wore a hat, and it didn't matter if his hair brushed the tops of his ears, but when he was in the regular world, he took time to make sure his thick, wavy hair was brushed back in a style somewhere between messy and too perfect.

Kind of the way he'd describe himself. A mess on the inside, but to the rest of the world, he tried to always present himself as confident and completely in control.

He wasn't giving up hope that Morgana would change her mind and agree to help him have an heir. A child of his bloodline who he would love in a way that his biological family had not. They hadn't loved him enough to keep him. It they had given him up at birth that would be one thing, but to abandon him as a toddler in a park…

He growled in disgust and pushed that old wound back where it belonged. Buried deep in a past that he hated looking back on. Tonight was all about the future, and enjoying the company of a beautiful woman. And convincing her they could make a good partnership. He shoved his wallet into his pocket, grabbed his keys and locked his motel room door. Part of his not-so-thought-out plan was to show Morgana what life could be like with a cool million or so in her account.

He grabbed the small gift he'd bought for Morgana because it had made him think of her, walked the few doors down to her room and knocked lightly. It swung open a few seconds later and his stomach flipped even though he'd just reminded himself about keeping any deep feelings out of the mix. Her hair that was usually pulled back in a ponytail flowed loose and full past her shoulders, and her vivid green eyes were enhanced with makeup.

"Wow. You're gorgeous, dancing queen."

"Thank you." She glanced down to adjust her silver chain belt and clutched tightly to a small green purse with her other hand.

He hated seeing her nervousness and wanted her to be relaxed. His goal was for her to be smiling and happy, not only because he wanted her to consider his proposal, but because she deserved to enjoy the evening. As well as maybe giving him a clue as to why she was in town and what she was really after. Because even though her desk held a laptop and a stack of notebooks, he didn't really think it was to write a book about old town history. She read fairytales, and there was a pile of romance novels on her dresser. It just didn't seem to fit her personality, but there was always a chance he could be wrong.

"Since you read all those Cinderella stories, I saw something that made me think of you and I bought them." He held up a pair of short socks that were made to look like a pair of baby blue glass slippers with a little pink bow on the toe.

"Oh, Bear. Those are so cute! Thank you. My very own glass slippers." She took them and held them to her chest like they were precious jewels.

"I'm glad you like them."

"I really do." She walked over to her bedside table and put them on top of her Cinderella book.

"Are you ready to go?"

"I'm ready." She smiled and some of her self-consciousness slipped away to reveal the gutsy woman he admired.

As they went down the stairs, he offered his arm, and she hesitated only a moment before curling her hand around his bicep.

"You look very handsome. I like that you are man enough to wear pink. It looks nice against your olive complexion."

"Thanks. That's what the lady at the store said. And I'm not ashamed to admit that I've always liked pink."

Morgana's arm jerked slightly against his, and he followed her gaze. Freya was standing near the bottom of the stairs, staring at them as she wrung her hands. She always seemed a little anxious, but tonight she was also agitated. Was it because they were together? Freya was likely worried that the motel maid was after his money and had no idea that he was the one who was after something in their relationship.

Relationship? No, no, no.

A slap of warning gripped him. Partnership or team or any number of things were a better way to describe what he wanted with Morgana.

"Hi, Mrs. Fortune," Morgana said.

"Where are you two going?" Freya asked.

He took the last step down. "To dinner at the LC Club."

"Together?" Freya's voice rose in pitch, giving away her concern. He wasn't completely sure why. Did she know something about Morgana that he didn't? Some reason that they shouldn't spend time together?

"Yes. Just the two of us. We have a lot to talk about." He said it to see how she would react, and when the lines of worry on her face deepened, it was telling. She was not happy about it.

"Oh. I see. Well, enjoy your evening out."

"Thanks," Morgana replied. "See you tomorrow."

"Have a good night." They walked away from his step-granny, and he didn't look back to see if she was still frowning at them. Freya and Morgana each had answers he wanted, and he was starting to feel like he was in a book or movie.

Now, the only thing to do was to wait and see whether it would be a comedy or a tragedy.

Chapter Seven

Once they were driving away from the motel and Freya was out of sight, Morgana relaxed into the leather seat. The radio was tuned to a classic rock station. It was her favorite era of music. Had she told him that or did he really like it, too? "What's your go-to music?"

"I like to change it up. Rock, country, blues and once in a while, heavy metal."

"That's a good mix. Freya likes to play jazz and sometimes big band music that makes you want to dance." She slid him a glance. "Speaking of Freya… did you get the feeling she was nervous about the two of us spending time together?"

"Yes. I got the same impression. She's clearly up to something, or worried about something."

"As much as I've tried over the months, I've barely gotten to know her. She's very private and dodges me most of the time."

"She won't give you an interview for your book?" he asked.

The muscles along her shoulders tensed, and she clasped her hands in her lap. "Nope."

She hated keeping Bear in the dark about who she was and the truth of why she was in Chatelaine, because despite what she'd told him, it wasn't by chance. She'd tasked herself with finding out what became of her long-estranged grandmother, discovering the truth behind the silver mine collapse and clearing the Wells family name.

He slowed as they neared a stop sign. "But she sure likes to be in other people's business."

"I'm sure your family has told you about the troubles many of them encountered when it came to the wish Freya was granting them. And before you ask, I know because your soon-to-be sister-in-law Haley told me."

"Is that so?" he asked.

"Yes. We've gotten to know one another over the months. We were working together on the mystery of the anonymous notes about the fifty-first miner until she made a decision to drop the story because she decided that her love for Camden was more important than writing an exposé for a newspaper."

"I'm glad to hear that she loves my brother that much. And now you've taken up where the two of you left off?"

She nodded. "Something like that."

"I do know that my cousin Asa ran into trouble buying Chatelaine Dude Ranch. Some craziness about him needing to be married to buy it."

"And then Bea's opening night of Cowgirl Café was a disaster with too many things going wrong at once to be considered coincidences," she added. She liked having someone to talk things over with again. She hadn't had that since Haley had decided she wanted nothing more to do with the whole mystery. But Morgana wasn't ready to give up.

"And just recently, my brother Camden had a lot of unexpected red tape getting his children's riding camp up and running. What do we actually know about my late grandfather Elias Fortune's widow?"

Morgana idly played with the star charm on her necklace. "Not as much as you'd think after all these months. I've wondered if she's been doing all this wish granting without having the noble intentions that she wants people to believe."

"Why in the world would she go to so much trouble to grant wishes for people she doesn't even know only to destroy them? It doesn't make sense," he said.

"Maybe that's what we should focus on. Why is she going to so much trouble for people she doesn't know? Did she love Elias that much? Could it be to make up for the harm Elias and Edgar Fortune caused years ago?"

"You mean the silver mine disaster?" Bear asked.

"Yes. Apparently, it's well known around town that they were responsible for the silver mine collapse and not the mine foreman, Clinton Wells. But no official statement has ever been made to clear the Wells name." All these years later, her grandfather was still officially taking the blame.

Bear's thumb tapped the steering wheel in time

to the upbeat song on the radio. "And then there are the two mysterious notes about how many died in the collapse."

She considered restating what each note said but mentioning her grandmother's name in the last one gave her pause. "I also have a collection of letters you might find interesting. Wendell gave them to me and Haley, and then when Haley decided she no longer wanted to pursue the story, she gave them all to me."

"Who are the letters from?" he asked.

"They're from Elias's secret daughter, Ariella."

He slowed to go around a curve in the lakeside road. "For real or is this your imagination adding to the story you want to write?"

Every time he mentioned her writing a book, another splash of guilt layered on like a thick coating of oil. She'd come up with that excuse on a whim and hated that she'd told him another lie. "A hundred percent real. Wendell had forbidden her to see the poor miner boyfriend she'd fallen in love with. In the last letter your great uncle said he'd read from her, Ariella admitted that she'd had a baby and was hiding the child, but it was time for her father to know the truth."

"Wow. My family has a lot of scandals and secrets. I would like to read the letters Wendell gave you."

"That's great. It will be more fun to have someone to talk to about it. You can be Watson to my Sherlock."

He gave her a playful scowl. "Why do *you* get to be Sherlock?"

"I think it's because…" She tapped a finger against her mouth. "Oh, I remember. Because I arrived in town before you."

"Hmm. Not sure that's very official, but I suppose we'll go with it."

"Excellent decision, Mr. Fortune. There is also a letter from Wendell to me and Haley in which he admits to being scandalized by his daughter's behavior—which seems a bit hypocritical if you ask me. Especially since she was a *secret* daughter."

"No doubt."

"Wendell assumes Ariella ran away with her baby after her miner boyfriend died. But he's not sure."

"So, one of the big questions is, what became of Elias's secret daughter, Ariella, and her child?"

On their drive from the motel to the lake, Bear had learned more about his family and some about Freya, but he had not gleaned anything new about Morgana. Although she seemed so real and authentic, he had a strong feeling there was something she was hiding—just like Freya seemed to be doing. After valet parking, he helped her out of the car and led her toward the entrance. He held open the door of the LC Club, and she went in ahead of him.

At his request when he'd called in the reservation, they were seated at a table for two in a secluded corner with a view of Chatelaine Lake. After pulling out her chair, he sat across from her. They could be somewhat alone while having the safety net of being in a public place. It wouldn't do anything to stave off his desire for her, but they were a whole lot safer in a public place than being in one of their motel rooms. Especially with the way she was nibbling one corner of her mouth, making her full lower lip even plumper. And driving him *crazy*.

"It's such a beautiful view," she murmured as she looked out the large wall of plate-glass windows. The water was calm and glistening as the sun crept toward the horizon.

He wanted to say she was more beautiful than the view but that sounded cliché, so he just agreed. "Do you drink wine?"

"Sometimes, but I know next to nothing about it, unless it has a screw top. Will you order for me?"

"Absolutely. I can do that." He liked that she was being herself and not pretending to be someone she wasn't. It was a refreshing change from a lot of the women he'd known and dated. His chest tightened as he caught his line of thinking.

We're not dating.

"Let's decide what we want to eat first, and then I'll know whether to order you red or white. I'm having steak. They make a great one here."

"Steak sounds wonderful. I haven't had one since… Gosh. A while now." She licked her lips as if anticipating the taste.

Once again drawing his eyes to her tempting mouth. If she kept up this level of unconscious seduction, he was going to have a hell of a time not finding out what she tasted like, even if they were in public. "Since we're both having beef, let's go with red wine. While I was in Brazil, I started drinking Malbec from the Mendoza region of Argentina. I think you'll like it."

She traced a finger along a line on the menu. "Will it go well with the charcuterie board?"

"For sure."

"Oh, good. It says the board is mostly locally sourced ingredients, and I'd love to sample what the area has to offer."

He grinned. "I'm glad to hear it. I was afraid you'd be shy about ordering or eating anything."

"I'm shy about some things, but food isn't one of them." She lowered her voice like it was a secret. "I like to watch cooking shows."

"I'm not much of a cook, but I'm right there with you on the eating part."

"I would cook something for you, but I'm pretty limited with my single hot plate and toaster oven," she confessed.

He was sad for her that she didn't have the kitchen to do something she enjoyed. Most of the places he'd rented recently had killer kitchens that he rarely used. This is why staying at the Chatelaine Motel was good for him. He sometimes took the luxuries his money afforded for granted.

The waiter returned, and he ordered the wine, appetizer and steak dinners. The bottle of wine came out quickly and he watched her closely as she took her first sip. He'd seen the contorted faces a person could make if they didn't like a wine, but Morgana's expression was delighted.

"Do you approve?"

"I do. It's smooth with such a nice aftertaste." She held up her glass to swirl the wine and see the color with the candlelight shining through. She knew more about wine than she realized.

He told her about wine tasting in different parts of the world and she asked questions about his travels. The artfully arranged charcuterie board arrived shortly after.

"Beautiful presentation." She studied the options.

"I'm about to mess it up because I'm starving."

"Go for it," she said with a laugh.

He popped a toasted pecan half into his mouth then grabbed a slice of salami and a cracker.

She spread soft, white cheese on a cracker, drizzled it with honey and took a bite. "Mmm. The goat cheese is delicious. Almost as good as mine."

"You know how to make goat cheese?"

"I do. On the farm where I grew up, my mom and I were the ones who made it."

This was the perfect opportunity to dig a little deeper into her life without his questions coming out of the blue. "Are you an only child?"

"Yes. It's always just been me and my mom."

"Tell me about what it was like to grow up on a farm in Tennessee. What were you like as a kid?

"A bit of a wild child. I ran around barefoot as much as I could in the summer, and when it was warm enough, I swam in the creek. The water comes from melting snow in the mountains and is pretty cold. My hair was really long, and I usually had a braid or two."

"Somehow, I can see all that about you," he said with a smile. "Did you have animals and a garden?"

"A huge garden and an orchard. I know I said it was just me and my mom, but we weren't the only ones living on the farm. It's more of a communal farm with several families all working together. But we do have our own little house where my mom still lives. We have a farm stand along the road where we sell the produce, honey, goat cheese and other hand-made goods."

"You had goats?" He popped an olive into his mouth.

"Yes. We also had chickens and a few dairy cows. Everyone had their jobs. My mom and I made the cheese and helped in the orchard, among other jobs, while others made the preserves and tended the bees and all the other farm stuff."

"It sounds like a storybook setting."

"There were times growing up when I thought it was so boring and such hard work, but looking back, it was a pretty great childhood." A wistful expression crossed her face. "Being an only child, I was some-times lonely for other kids. I bet it's nice having broth-ers."

"It is. We looked out for one another while we were growing up."

"You're the oldest brother, right?" she asked.

"Yes. At thirty-two, I'm a year older than West and three older than Camden."

"Were you too young to remember when they were born? I always wanted a baby sister or brother. I love babies."

He liked hearing her say that about babies. It could help with his idea for her to have one, or it could backfire and be the reason she wouldn't have one *for him*. "West was already born when I was adopted."

"I didn't realize you were adopted. I guess that answers the question about why you don't look much like your brothers."

Bear hadn't meant to reveal so much. He didn't like talking about the past, especially his origin story. Sometimes he wondered if there was something about him that was unlovable. Why else would his birth family abandon him and then his wife climb into bed with his best friend? He pushed those thoughts aside and refocused on Morgana and the present moment. He was supposed to be getting her to talk about herself and not bemoaning about his painful past.

"West and Camden aren't lucky enough to have my dark good looks."

She swirled her wine and grinned. "Or your wonderful sense of modesty, I'm sure."

"Oh, of course. That goes without saying." He refilled her wine glass, and they continued their easy conversation with lots of laughter.

Even though his family hadn't been perfect, he was grateful to have been adopted as a toddler by Peter and Dolly Fortune. However, he reminded himself that part of the reason he wanted a biological child of his own was because he had no blood relatives. He wanted to look into eyes that shared a piece of his DNA.

How to make that happen without involving his heart was the ever-present question. He'd been harshly fooled by love and had no plans to repeat it.

Morgana savored every bite of delicious food, and the wine—which was starting to make her giggly— was the best she'd ever had. Their date that she'd worried would be awkward was going really well. Almost *too* well. She was so attracted to Bear. He was engaging and smart and funny and kind, even if he did have a nutty idea about her having his baby.

As they walked from the restaurant out into the starry night, keeping her identity a secret for a moment longer felt wrong. "Can we take a walk along the lake path before we go home? I have something I'd like to tell you."

"Sure. A walk sounds good."

They fell into step, and when she slipped on loose gravel, he reached out and steadied her. But instead of letting go, he slid his fingers slowly down the inside of her arm, leaving a trail of tingly sensations. His hand was warm and strong and comforting, but it wasn't as soft as she would've guessed. This wealthy businessman had calluses from some type of manual labor, but his nails were well manicured. Barrington Fortune was a contradiction she hadn't figured out, but she planned to do just that, and if it continued like this, it would be a lot of fun.

His thumb stroked the back of her hand in a lover's caress, but just when she thought they would walk hand in hand, he let go. And she instantly missed his touch.

Oh, boy. This level of infatuation could be a real problem.

She forced a smile. "Thanks for the save."

"Anytime." They began to walk along the winding pathway beside the lake. A light breeze blew across the water and carried the scent of damp soil. "What is it you wanted to tell me?"

"Since I arrived here in Chatelaine, I've been keeping a secret, and I haven't had anyone to talk to about it." She hadn't missed the way he stiffened at her words, but she couldn't continue to keep her identity hidden. Not with the way she felt about him.

"You can talk to me," he said.

"I just have one request. Will you promise to keep my secret for the time being?"

He studied her for a long moment. "If it's not hurting anyone, then yes, I will."

She took a deep breath and looked up to meet his curious gaze. "My real last name isn't Mills. It's Wells. Morgana Wells."

"*Wells.* Why is that familiar?" Before she could answer, his eyes widened. "Like as in Clint Wells? The mine foreman?"

"Yes. The one who was unfairly blamed for the mine collapse. He was my grandfather."

Bear stopped walking and shook his head like he was searching for answers. "The man who my grandfather Elias and his brother Edgar Fortune blamed for the mine disaster that killed fifty or more people?"

She was suddenly cold and wrapped her arms around herself. "Yes, from my research, that is what I believe to be true."

"Are you here because you want something from the Fortune family? Money? Revenge?"

She gasped and took a step back. "No! I want nothing more than answers." Only a few hours ago, he'd been the one who said she wasn't a woman motivated by money. Especially since she'd declined the million-dollar offer to have his baby. But she wasn't about to become a rich man's baby mama. Not for any price. "Revenge is what tore my family apart, and I'm trying to put it back together."

He raked his fingers through his hair. "Will you tell me more about what's motivating you then?"

"I'm here in Chatelaine looking for clues about what became of my grandmother, Gwenyth Wells. That's why I've been asking so many questions. I only want to reunite my long-estranged family. And if possible, clear the Wells family name."

Even in the light of the crescent moon, she could see the hesitancy playing across his handsome face. Her throat tightened. Had she made a mistake in revealing her identity?

Chapter Eight

Bear had learned to read people, but from the moment he found her dancing on his bed, Morgana had enchanted and intrigued him. He searched her face, and his tight lungs began to unlock. Gorgeous green eyes met his without a hint of shame, and her body language wasn't shrinking in on oneself like people did when they were lying or holding back. Her arms were held out and her palms up in an open, honest posture as if to say, *See me. All of me. I'm laying it all out for you.*

"Bear, I have no need of vengeance."

"I believe you."

He couldn't resist stroking her cheek with the back of his fingers and was pleased when the tension left her face. Bear could usually spot someone trying to fool him during a business deal, and Morgana wasn't one of those people. She was tough and spunky and being honest with him. And there wasn't a doubt in his mind that she also knew how to stand up for herself. So maybe there was a chance she would be able to handle an agreement to have a mutually beneficial partnership?

"Fair warning, though," she said. "The grandmother who I'm looking for is a whole different story. It was Gwenyth's all-consuming desire for vengeance that drove my mom to leave at the age of eighteen and start over in Tennessee. She made a life for herself and then for me, far away from the stress of her mother's vendetta."

"Your mom must be a brave woman."

"She is."

"I'm glad you told me your secret," he said.

"Me, too. It feels good to tell someone, and I want you to know the real me." The pea gravel crunched softly under her feet as she turned back toward the restaurant. "And one other thing. Although I am doing a lot of research, I'm not actually writing a book."

Bear grinned at her. "I had a suspicion, but I bet you could write a book if you wanted to."

He held out his elbow, and she hooked her arm through his as they walked back toward his car. He was surprised by her reveal, but she was so sincere about her reasons. And he could relate to wanting information about relatives you've never met. After Peter and Dolly found him abandoned at the playground, the police hit a dead end in finding his parents or any other blood relatives. But there had to be someone out there in the world who knew where he'd come from.

Morgana now knew that the Fortunes adopted him, and she might have told him her secret, but he hated his origins and had never confided the whole story. Not to anyone.

Now who's the one holding back and being deceptive? I'm a hypocrite.

A cool night breeze blew across the water and tossed Morgana's long hair against his shoulder, and she tucked it behind her ear. "I've been worried that if anyone discovers my true identity that they'll try to block me from finding out any more information and ruin my chances of finding my grandmother. Or what might have become of her." She sighed. "I don't even know if she's alive. She may have died years ago, but there's no record. It's like she disappeared from the face of the earth. I might be chasing a ghost."

The look of sadness on her face tugged at his suddenly vulnerable heart, and he pulled her into a hug. They swayed together in the dark while crickets and frogs at the water's edge sang their night songs. Her determination to find her grandmother made him reconsider searching for his birth family, but he immediately pushed the idea away. He had no interest in the long-ago past. There was no changing it, so what did it matter.

Tonight had started with the goal of convincing Morgana to have a baby for him—which he wasn't completely giving up on—as well as learning more about her. The evening had yielded more information than he'd expected, but their time together had also done something else that was not on the approved list. It had brought them closer.

"Have you given any more thought to forming a mutually beneficial partnership and having a baby?"

She gave him a melancholy look. "I'm not having a baby unless it's with someone I love."

It shouldn't come as a surprise that a woman like her wanted love and not money, but he couldn't afford to fall for the woman who gave birth to his child. And truth be told, he was starting to care about Morgana.

Well hell. This is less than ideal.

He was being cynical, which was all the more reason to keep his heart out of things. And protect hers. She wasn't willing to be the mother of his child, and he was coming to quickly realize that was probably a good thing.

On the drive back to the motel, they talked about music and books and movies. All safe topics. They discovered a mutual enjoyment of classic movies that had been made around the time the Chatelaine Motel was built.

Bear extended a hand to help Morgana out of his car and considered keeping it clasped with his, but he forced himself to let his fingers slide from hers. "I'll walk you to your door."

"Oh, my. I couldn't ask you to go so far out of your way," she teased as they made their way toward the stairs.

"It's my pleasure." He internally groaned. Why had he used the word *pleasure*? Now that's exactly what he wanted to give both of them.

He briefly squeezed his eyes closed as they stopped

in front of her room. While she unlocked her door, he shoved his hands in the front pockets of his slacks in an effort to resist pulling her into his arms again. Because this time he might not want to stop.

Make sure she's safely inside, say good night and walk away.

"Thank you so much for the wonderful dinner and for listening to me." She placed her hand flat on his chest. "You have a good heart. Use it to really think about how you want your future to look. As for me… A baby would be a part of me, and I know that I could never accept anything less than being a full-time parent."

A sinking feeling settled hard and heavy in his stomach, and he knew Morgana would not be the mother of his child. "I understand."

But spending some time with her wouldn't hurt anything. He covered her hand with his and then brought it to his mouth to kiss her palm. When she swayed in his direction and grasped the front of his shirt, all his reasons for holding back evaporated in a cloud of mingled pheromones.

Like a synchronized dance, they were in one another's arms, and all he knew was the sweet warmth of her mouth. Her hands in his hair and his on her back, tracing the soft bumps of her spine. The chemistry flaring between them was more intoxicating than any wine. More powerful than he'd expected.

But then a car door slammed, reminding him they were outside—where anyone could see them.

* * *

Morgana grasped his shoulders to steady herself. She saw her own surprise reflected in his dazed expression. Neither of them had been prepared for the sensual power of their first kiss. Her skin buzzed and delicious pressure built low in her body.

"Bear." Her voice was almost a whisper.

"Yes, sweetheart?"

"How much longer will you be in Chatelaine?" she asked.

"Probably a few more weeks."

That seemed like the perfect amount of time to have a short love affair and not get so attached that it hurt too much when it was over. She summoned up her big girl courage and decided to go for it. "Want to hang out with me until you go?"

His grin started at one corner of his mouth and spread into a full-watt smile. "That's an excellent idea."

Ask him to come in. A caution alarm clanged in her head. *Not yet! Too soon.*

"I'm glad we're in agreement," she said. "I'll see you tomorrow."

"Yes, you will."

She went up on her toes and kissed him, nipping ever so lightly on his lower lip. He made a very satisfied masculine sound deep in his throat. A shiver of anticipation zipped through her, and she took several backward steps into her room to keep herself from pulling him inside. Because she had no doubt he'd come willingly. "I had a wonderful time. Good night, Bear."

"Sweet dreams, dancing queen."

She closed the door and then walked to the center of her room, unsure what to do next. She wasn't the least bit sorry she'd decided to spend time with Bear. She might be tipsy from the wine, but she was drunk on his kiss. And excited and eager to see what came next for them. She spun to swirl her skirt like she'd always done when her mom made her a new dress and she felt pretty. Bear made her feel pretty and desirable in a way she'd never experienced.

She hit Play on the old CD player she kept on her dresser. The one people teased her for still using, but she had a collection of CDs that she still loved to listen to. The first song off of *ABBA Gold: Greatest Hits* played softly as she undressed and took off her makeup. Because of Bear's nickname for her, "Dancing Queen" was her new favorite song.

She considered calling her mom to tell her about her date, but it was too late. Renee Wells was an early-to-bed and early-to-rise kind of person. She missed their in-person talks and wished she wasn't so far away. Even though her mom had worried about her setting off from a farm in rural Tennessee in a rattly old car and not much money, she hadn't been able to resist the allure of adventure.

And she had a strong feeling that Barrington Fortune was going to be one hell of an adventure.

Chapter Nine

Alone in his motel room, Bear lay on the surprisingly comfortable mattress staring at the ceiling. The power of Morgana's kiss had done something unexpected to him. It had become an instant addiction. A craving he couldn't stop thinking about.

Thank goodness she wasn't clingy or instantly talking about *couple* stuff. She had been the one to ask him to hang out *until* he left, and that was a huge relief. There was an end date to their time together. And that was a really good thing, because after hearing the awful story of Wendell's secret illegitimate daughter, he was less inclined than ever to bring romance and love into the equation. Ariella hiding a secret, forbidden love and a baby, and then her boyfriend being killed in the mine was all so tragic and sad. Ariella's child would be in her late fifties now. Had mother and baby run off after the mine disaster just like Morgana's mom had done?

His logical brain knew he had to go the surrogacy route, but there was an ornery-as-hell part of him that wanted Morgana to be the mother of his child. Could it be done without hurting her?

Impossible.

Hurting her was as likely as the sun rising and setting. He needed to stop torturing himself with the idea of her pregnant with his child.

With a growl, he rolled onto his side for a different view. A thin ribbon of moonlight sliced through the gap in the curtains. It made him think of their walk beside the lake. Her vulnerability was endearing, but also a sign he needed to be careful with her young heart.

There was only one thing to do. He would find a surrogate like Morgana had suggested. Using someone he didn't have a relationship with to have his heir was really the best route to take. Just a contractual agreement, legal, nothing personal about it. No muss, no fuss.

The next day, someone knocked on Morgana's door and her first thought was that it was Bear, and her pulse began to speed up. "I have such a major crush on him," she whispered to herself on the way to her door.

The man she saw through the peephole was not her sexy neighbor, but instead, a man in his eighties—but she was glad to see him as well. He had something she needed.

Information.

"Hi, Wendell."

"Hello, Morgana. I have something for you."

She held the door open wider. "Please, come inside."

He eased himself onto the desk chair that Morgana pulled out for him and rubbed a weathered hand against his denim-covered thigh. "I'll get straight to the point. I found the missing letter from Ariella."

"Oh, that's good news!"

"I set it aside decades ago because I couldn't bring myself to read it. Then a couple of days ago, I found it in the back of a desk drawer. When I pulled it out, I remembered it arriving the day after the mine collapsed. I assumed it was a letter blaming me for the death of the man she loved, and that she never wanted to see me again. I guess I also worried it was something I wouldn't want to know. There was so much going on. I shoved it in a drawer and forgot about it."

"What does it say? Did she run off with the baby?"

When Wendell cleared his throat and gave the slightest shake of his head, she granted him a moment to collect himself. She sat on her bed beside her laundry basket of clean clothes and casually pulled out a pair of shorts and started folding them as if she had nothing but time.

"I don't know what it says. It's still sealed." From his shirt pocket, he pulled out an envelope, yellowed and crumpled with age. "You take it."

"Are you sure? We can read it together if you want."

He shook his head again and put it on her desk. With a hand braced on the corner, he pushed himself up with a wince. "I'm sure. I need to go. Take care of yourself, young lady."

"You, too, Wendell."

Her heart was racing as she closed the door behind him. This letter from Ariella could be an important clue. She sat on her bed to open it but first held it against her chest and said a silent prayer that it held some of the answers she'd been searching for, and for Wendell to have some peace.

She slid her finger under the envelope flap, the old glue dried out and easily giving way. The thick paper crinkled as she unfolded it. The first thing she looked at was the date in the top right corner, and an electric jolt sizzled through her.

"That's the day of the mine collapse!"

Dear Father,
By the time you get this letter, my fiancé and I will be long gone. I'm sorry you don't approve of my choices, but tonight, I'm leaving our baby girl with a sitter while I go into the mine to get the man I love, and then we plan to elope. I'll contact you once we are married and settled and see if you want to meet your granddaughter. And if you've forgiven me.

"Oh, no." Morgana's hand flew to her mouth, and a spiderweb of chills raced across her skin. "She went into the mine the night of the collapse. Ariella Fortune must be the fifty-first miner."

The short letter hadn't revealed anything about Gwenyth, but big wow. She had discovered the identity of the fifty-first miner. Wendell was such a sweet elderly man who'd been through so much. "How can I tell him that his daughter most likely died that night?"

With a heavy heart and cheeks streaked with mascara, Morgana folded it neatly and put it back into its envelope where it had been for almost fifty years She had to tell Wendell before Haley or any of the other Fortunes. Although, there was one member of the Fortune family she could go to. Bear had become her confidant. They'd come to an agreement to share and keep one another's secrets. He wouldn't spread the news around before Wendell knew. And she really needed to talk to someone about this.

She cleaned up her smudged makeup and then went to see if Bear was in his room. She knocked and heard movement before the door opened.

"Hi…" His wide smile dropped away. "What's wrong? Come inside."

She rushed past him, clutching the old handwritten letter in her hand. "I made a discovery."

"Sit, sweetheart, and tell me what's going on." He patted the foot of the bed, and she sat beside him.

"Wendell finally found the missing letter from his secret daughter, Ariella." She held it up like it was Exhibit A. "His daughter was the fifty-first miner." A fresh tear slid down her cheek.

Bear wiped it away with his thumb. "How can that be?"

"Read it." She watched his facial expression rapidly change as he read. "Pretty shocking, isn't it? And so sad. Young love tragically lost. At least they were together at the end, hopefully in one another's arms. At least that's what I'm choosing to believe." She sniffed and wiped away a few more tears.

He put the letter aside, drew her into his arms and they lay back on the bed with her head on his shoulder. "I wonder what happened to the baby?"

She sighed, settling herself against his side and taking the comfort he offered. "This brings up so many new questions. Who raised the baby, and does she have any idea she's a Fortune?"

"I don't understand why the babysitter wouldn't come forward and say she had Ariella's baby."

"I guess it's possible Ariella didn't tell the sitter the identity of the father, or maybe whoever it was felt too intimidated to tell Wendell Fortune. So many unanswered questions. It's all so tragic." She stroked her fingers across his chest as they talked, absentmindedly exploring the dips and planes of his muscles through the soft fabric of his pinstriped dress shirt.

"It makes you stop and think. After believing for so long that West was dead, I have a new appreciation for how quickly things can be taken from you. You never know when it might be the last time you see someone."

She propped herself up on her elbow so she could see him. He was so handsome. So irresistible. "I guess the lesson is not to waste time and miss out on living?"

"That sounds right to me." He sat up to face her and cradled the back of her head, massaging her scalp and drawing her slowly closer. "What should we do about this idea of not missing out? Any thoughts?"

Showing him seemed a much better option than telling, and she couldn't wait another nanosecond for his kiss. Closing the small distance between them, she meant for it to be a soft, teasing caress, but when he slid the tip of his tongue between her lips, she lost her very thin hold over her good girl self-control. Their kiss became deep and searching as they fell into perfect rhythm.

He kissed a path along the curve of her neck and across her collarbone. "You have the most gorgeous shoulders. Do you want to know one of the things I find so sexy about you?"

"Tell me," she said, her voice sounding breathy.

"Your eagerness for adventure," he rasped, then rolled them until she straddled his hips.

As she looked down into Bear's mesmerizing dark eyes, *eager* was an excellent way to describe her current feelings. So were *excited* and *enthusiastic*.

She began to slowly unbutton his shirt. "Do you feel like having an adventure right now?"

"That's a brilliant idea." His hands slid along her thighs, and she shivered under his touch. "Let the adventure begin."

Morgana slept in his arms after proving his theory that their passion would be fireworks. Her soft hair was fanned across his chest, and he trailed his fingers through its silkiness. Bear waited for the usual urge to get up and dressed and put necessary space between himself and the woman in his bed. But the urge never came. In fact, the impulse that filled him was to wake her up, make love to her again and hold her all night long.

An uncomfortable current of caution surged across his skin, and he flinched. She shifted and mumbled something in her sleep that he didn't understand. This was the perfect time to get out of bed, but they were in his room. He should wake her up, but kicking her out felt all wrong. Next time they could go to her room, and then he'd be able to slip out of bed and go back to his own.

For tonight, though, Bear stayed right where he was, kissed the top of her head and held her a little tighter, letting his fingers play among the silky strands of her hair and lulling her back into a deep sleep. She didn't need to know that he was having a moment of weakness with a touch of freak-out.

Damn it. This is exactly what was not supposed to happen.

Morgana was still riding on the delicious high from waking up in Bear's arms that morning, and she couldn't wait for the next time they could hang out.

She was behind the motel's front desk while Hal ran some errands when a delivery arrived. The driver brought in several large boxes.

"I'm sorry one of the boxes got torn open a bit."

He pulled back a flap of cardboard. "It doesn't look damaged, but do you want to open it and check?"

"Sure. I can do that." She grabbed a pair of scissors and cut more of the packing tape. "Oh, it's a new housekeeping cart. It looks like it's completely undamaged."

"Very good. Have a nice day, miss."

"You, too." Morgana went back to finishing unboxing the shiny new housekeeping cart, and then tested it out around the small lobby. The wheels rolled smoothly, nothing rattled and there was more room on it than the old ones.

The lobby door opened again, and her boss came in with a bag of groceries.

"Hal, thanks for buying new housekeeping carts."

"What carts?" He glanced between the boxes and the one she was pushing around. "I didn't order these. I wonder if they were delivered to the wrong place?"

"I don't think so. It's your name and this address on the labels."

"Curious." He rubbed a hand over his belly that was straining the buttons of his shirt.

Morgana smiled and gave the cart another roll around the lobby as if she was a kid with a brand-new toy. "I have a pretty good idea where these came from. I think one of our guests ordered these."

"You think Mrs. Fortune bought them?"

"No. I think *Mr.* Fortune did." Her temporary knight in designer armor.

* * *

The night before, Bear had slept better with Morgana in his bed than he had in months. Maybe years. All morning he'd been telling himself his restful night was only because it had been so long since he'd been with a woman, and he'd exhausted himself.

Morgana was young and an ardent lover. She also had a deeply romantic heart that hadn't yet been touched by heartache like his. She thought she knew, but she had no idea how bad it could be. Just last night, she'd cried about the young lovers who'd died in the mine disaster decades ago. If she had his baby she would want—and rightly expect—more than he could give.

Making love with Morgana had been incredible. Also, an incredibly risky move, but it hadn't been a mistake. How could he ever regret experiencing the chemistry they had together?

As if there wasn't already a long list of reasons, this was even more confirmation that she could not have his baby. He couldn't afford to have strong romantic feelings for the mother of his child, and he wouldn't be able to separate his feelings if he had a child with Morgana. What if they started fighting like his parents had? If they were together and then at some point they weren't, the baby would be shuffled back and forth between parents. Then his child would grow up in a broken home. But wait—

It would be worse than that because she'd told him there was no way she would give up custody.

Bear sat back down at the small desk in the corner of his motel room, opened his laptop and started doing serious research about surrogacy. He read articles and scoured countless agency websites. Once he'd made a long bullet-point list of all the most important things, he decided which agency he would call first. The ball was rolling, and all that remained to be seen was if it would be a winning goal or if it would roll back downhill and crush him flat.

A tiny voice inside him continued to whisper that Morgana should be the mother of his child, but without the heart involved.

Still impossible just like it was a few hours ago, bonehead. Why do I keep tormenting myself by even thinking about it?

She was also too tenderhearted to be a friends-with-benefits kind of woman. She deserved so much more than that. More than he had to give.

Someone knocked, and he yelled out for them to come in because he needed a distraction from his own thoughts.

Morgana opened the door. "Oh, sorry. It looks like I caught you right in the middle of something. I'll come back later."

"Stay." It was then that he recognized the calming effect she brought into a room—like a Disney princess with a halo of birds and small woodland creatures gathered near. He looked around at his scattered handwritten notes and crumpled wads of paper. Now was the perfect time to make sure she knew he was serious about his plans to have an heir. It would put some necessary space between them, because he could not allow himself to get used to having her in his daily life. "I was doing some research, and I'd like to tell you about it."

She easily pulled her housekeeping cart over the threshold and into the room. "How do you like my shiny new cart?"

"Very nice. Where did you get it?"

"I believe I have a secret admirer who wants to make my life a little easier. I think I'll find a creative way to thank them."

He returned her smile. "Sounds like a hell of a guy."

"How do you know it's a guy?"

"Just a hunch."

She came around behind him to see what he was doing and rested her hands on his shoulders.

He knew the second she saw the surrogacy website pulled up on the screen. Her fingers suddenly flexed against the tense muscles on each side of his neck.

He was doing this to protect her as well as himself. "I'm going to find an egg donor and a surrogate to have my child."

Chapter Ten

The light and cheery feeling of happiness that had put extra pep in Morgana's steps all day suddenly drained out as if someone had pulled a plug.

She slipped her hands from Bear's shoulders and clasped them behind her back so she wouldn't be tempted to touch him. The surrogacy website Bear was looking at was a giant flashing billboard announcing he was going ahead with his wacky plan, and he didn't see her in his future. Which he'd told her repeatedly, but apparently she wasn't very good at listening.

"You're really going to do it? You're going to hire a surrogate to have a baby for you?"

"I don't see any other way."

She walked over to his bed and sat down. "I think you're missing the whole point of it all."

He shook his head and ran a hand roughly through his hair. "I assure you I'm not. My point is, romantic love leads to disaster and estrangement."

"Not always. Love and family and sharing the joys and struggles of life with a partner can be wonderful. Watching your child grow and sharing the good as well as the difficult parts of being a parent. Supporting one another." Her mom had been a single mother, and Morgana had seen her struggles, and she didn't want that for herself or for Bear.

"I have something that can help. Money. I can hire the best to help me."

She ducked her head, letting her hair screen her face because she knew her expression would give away her disappointment. Not to mention the disapproval of his plan. "Are you going to go the rest of your life without loving a woman?"

"That's the plan." He crossed his arms over his chest and leaned back in the chair.

She suddenly felt cold and tucked her feet beneath her. From the things he'd previously said, she got the impression there were painful things in Bear's past that he didn't like to talk about, and she wasn't sure if now was the right time to question him about it. "That sounds...lonely."

"I didn't say I wasn't going to date and have casual connections."

Casual connections? Tension banded her chest. *That must be what I am to him.*

Of course it was. She was a temporary fling to him, but she had herself to blame because she'd been the one who suggested *hanging out* until he left town. She would have to seriously sort through all these feelings. Soon. "Oh, Bear. Who hurt you?"

He scratched his head and looked like he was making up his mind about something important. "I have an ex-wife. We were married a few years and then she and my best friend thought it would be a good idea to hook up when I was out of town on business."

"Damn. That's harsh."

"Do you know what's even harsher? Walking in on them."

Morgana winced. "I'm so sorry that happened to you."

"I lost a wife *and* a friend that day," he bit out.

"And you've lost your parents, too?"

"Yes, five years ago in a plane crash with my aunt and uncle."

Morgana wanted to go to him, but with his arms crossed so protectively over his body, she wasn't sure if he wanted her affection or not. "There are people who will stick by you and not break your heart. I've seen you with your family. You told me you were adopted, so that means the Fortunes wanted you."

"It's a little more complicated than that." He rubbed a hand over his face, tapped his bare foot on the floor and then came over to sit beside her on his bed. "When I was a toddler, Peter and Dolly Fortune found me sitting alone in a sandbox at a park."

Her breath snagged, but she managed to control her reaction. At least she hoped she'd hidden her shock. Silently, she put a hand on top of his and scooted closer to him.

"They looked for my family, but the police concluded I had been abandoned. They couldn't find my parents or any relatives, so the Fortunes took me in. West and I bonded quickly, and they adopted me."

She laced their fingers and leaned her head against his shoulder. "I know you might think it's cheesy to say, but they weren't forced to take you. They *chose* you to be part of their family."

He tipped up her chin and kissed her softly. "I guess you're right."

"I'm right a lot of the time. It happens quite frequently," she said with a smile, lightening the mood.

"I can believe that, sweetheart."

"Have you tried to find your birth family since then?"

He shook his head.

"Well, if you wanted to, you could get a 411 Me DNA kit and see if you have any matches. I bet you would have at least cousins who might know something."

"I've thought about it. That's how my cousin Esme found out her baby had been switched at birth." A shadow crossed his face and he muttered, "But I'm not sure I want to. I don't need to search them out and hear a sob story or an excuse about why they didn't want to keep me."

She decided not to push the issue. "I heard about the babies being switched. What a relief Esme and Ryder got that figured out, fell in love and are raising the baby boys as brothers."

"Was Freya around when that happened?" he asked. "The switching babies part."

She thought back over all the information she'd gathered. "Yes. She was already in town. It's another weird thing that has happened while Freya is here granting wishes on behalf of her late husband, Elias Fortune."

Bear rolled his neck as if his muscles had suddenly tensed. "But from what the others have told me, my step-granny is the one who gave Esme the DNA kit. If she had something to do with the babies being switched, why would she have done that?"

"Good question. Maybe because of guilt for doing something wrong?" she said.

"Could be, I guess."

She stood and walked to her cart. "I better get your room cleaned."

"I only need towels." He leaned back on his elbows. "And a roll of toilet paper."

"Very funny." She grabbed a roll and tossed it at him. She loved this playful side of him.

"How many more rooms do you have after mine?"

"Yours is the last one."

He lay all the way back on the bed with his hands under his head and flashed a big grin. "Saving the best for last?"

"Something like that. Then I'll figure out what to do with the rest of my day. There are just so many options, and I can't decide…"

"You know, now that I think about it, my shower needs cleaning, and I've heard that it's easier to clean if you do it while you are actually taking a shower," he said.

She flashed him a cheeky smile. "If that's what you heard, then it must be true. Want to help me test the theory?"

"Do you really have to ask?" He rose from the bed and pulled his T-shirt over his head.

She admired the defined muscles of his back as she followed him into the bathroom and closed the door.

For several days they hung out with one another as much as possible in between work and his family obligations. One Sunday morning, they were snuggled together in her bed watching TV when there was an advertisement for the day's 1980s movie marathon.

Morgana propped herself up so she could see Bear. "Since I have the day off, want to stay in bed all day, eat takeout and junk food while watching movies that became classics before we were born?"

He chuckled and kissed the pulse point on her wrist. "Sweetheart, you had me at stay in bed all day."

"Even though the first two movies they're showing are *Sixteen Candles* and *Say Anything*?"

"Is *Say Anything* the one where John Cusack holds up the big boom box like the one you have on your dresser?" He pointed to her CD player that wasn't nearly as big as the one in the movie.

"Hey, funny guy, mine isn't that big, but yes, that is the movie. My mom loves it, and I used to watch it with her."

"I'm going to call the café and get an order delivered. What would you like?" he asked.

"The ricotta pancakes with lemon curd and an order of bacon, please."

"Bacon always sounds good."

She was in the bathroom brushing her teeth when she heard him placing the order, and she almost choked on toothpaste when she started laughing about his last request. She rinsed her mouth and climbed back into bed. "Did you order a side of chocolate sauce from the Cowgirl Café?"

"I did." He propped himself up against the headboard, the sheet pooling in his lap. "You never know when it might come in handy."

The day went by in a happy blur of laughter, food, making love and a long leisurely shower after he'd had chocolate sauce for dessert—right off the most sensitive skin of her belly.

Morgana grabbed her keys and headed out to the parking lot to get something out of her car's trunk, but when she stood in front of the spot where it had been parked, it was empty. Her heart plummeted to the ground.

"Oh my God. Someone stole my car." She turned in a circle, just in case she'd forgotten where she parked. But Pumpkin was nowhere to be seen. "Why would anyone steal a car as old and rundown as mine?"

She had almost saved enough to fix it, but she certainly didn't have enough for a new car. Even another old clunker. She stood frozen in place for another minute. What was she supposed to do now? Live forever in the Chatelaine Motel? Her heart began to race.

"Morgana, what's wrong, kid?" Rhonda asked as she walked up beside her, with her own keys in her hand—which belonged to a car that was thankfully still parked in its spot.

"My car. It's gone! Someone stole it."

Her sassy coworker propped a hand on her hip. "What do you mean? I just saw your car this morning on the way to work."

That surprised her. "You did? Where?"

"At the mechanic shop. They had it on a lift and were underneath working on it."

"Oh. Really?" Morgana tried to make sense of it all. How had her car gotten across town? It wasn't even running.

"You didn't know it was there?"

"No. Maybe Hal got tired of it collecting dust in his parking lot and had it towed over to the mechanic and convinced them to give me credit."

Rhonda laughed. "Honey, I think you might have a knight in shining armor. And their name is definitely not Hal. Sorry, but I've gotta run. I'm late for an appointment."

"See you tomorrow," Morgana called after her and then turned back to the empty parking spot.

Bear Fortune. Did you do this like you did with the new carts?

A smile pulled up the corners of her mouth, but

then she glanced toward Freya's room. Had she done it? That was highly unlikely. The woman would hardly even talk to her, and Morgana wasn't one of the Fortunes who were getting their greatest wishes granted. There would be no reason for Freya to help the stranger who was always asking too many questions.

Morgana went straight to the lobby, and when Hall knew nothing about her car, it reinforced her hunch as to the identity of her benefactor.

Bear had gone somewhere with one of his brothers, and she didn't want to interrupt their time together, so she dismissed the idea of calling him. Reading her new romance novel sounded like a good way to pass the time waiting for Bear to get home. She came to a stop and pressed the heel of one hand to the knot in her chest.

This isn't home for either of us.

Nothing about this situation was permanent or lasting. He would leave first, and at some point, so would she. If she had a car when the time came.

Some people might be mad at him for making a decision about their car without asking, but she wasn't. Although, she did have to wonder about his motive. Was it another attempt at convincing her to have a baby for him? She would be disappointed if that was the case. He knew how she felt, and he was very clear about what he did and didn't want.

More likely, it was the generosity she'd witnessed. Like the time he left a thousand-dollar tip for the young waiter at the LC Club with a note telling him good luck at college. She doubted he would let her repay him, but that didn't mean she couldn't do something nice for him. She'd have to think of a few ideas.

When he drove up a while later, she closed her book and waved to him from the outdoor seating area. "You'll never guess what happened," she said as he got close. "My car was stolen."

"Is that right?" He grinned, and that told her everything she needed to know.

"Might you be the one who stole it, Mr. Fortune?"

"Guilty as charged, but I do plan to bring it back to you in better shape than it was."

"That won't be hard to do." She took his hand and started leading him upstairs. "But seriously, I really do appreciate the help. Thank you."

"You're welcome."

"Can I ask you why you did it?"

He followed Morgana into her room and closed the door behind them. "It was something that needs doing, and I have the means to get it done. Everyone deserves to have someone help them out now and then."

"My mom would adore you." She held her next breath and turned to put her book on the nightstand. This anti-committed-relationship guy probably didn't go for meeting parents.

"Moms always love me," he bragged and wrapped her in an embrace that made her shiver.

Relieved he wasn't getting twitchy about her comment, she kissed the strong line of his jaw. "I can believe that."

"Would you like to go to the lake with me tomorrow afternoon?"

"That sounds fun. I'd love to go," Morgana said.

"Cool. I was hoping you'd say yes. I rented a boat, and it has a cabin with a bed."

Her smile grew as tingles spread through her core. "How convenient. It must be a big boat."

"Not really. But it's big enough for an adventure."

"You know I'm up for an adventure anytime. You're spoiling me."

He swayed them gently from side to side. "Right again, dancing queen. It makes me happy to do it."

"So glad I can give you pleasure."

That earned her a kiss that demonstrated the fact. At first, she'd thought Bear was a playboy, but that was only surface-level camouflage. This smart, thoughtful, funny man knew what he was doing in the bedroom, and since both of their rooms had a bed smack-dab in the middle, they often found themselves in it.

"How do you feel about staying overnight on the boat?" he asked.

Her eyes widened. "Can we really do that?"

"Yes, we can."

"Well, in that case, I'm in. I guess we'll need to take food."

"We can order food from the café and stop by

GreatStore if we need to. Pack a swimsuit and... that's about it."

She rested her head against his chest and made up her mind to enjoy her time with him—while she could.

Chapter Eleven

Morgana stepped down into the boat's cabin. "Wow! This is so much nicer than I expected. How did you even know you could rent something like this?"

Bear had learned that for the right price, you could rent luxury almost anywhere. "It's easy when you have a great assistant who is good at finding things. He handles leasing and booking hotels, condos, flights, cars and all the logistics."

"Very handy."

He was pleased with the boat he'd rented. It was a small but beautiful overnight cabin cruiser with a tiny bathroom. The private boat dock was in the affluent area of Chatelaine Lake. Located in a secluded cove, it would allow them to have a peaceful night alone. He dropped their overnight bags onto the bed.

If she was interested, he could tell her about some of his adventures. Scuba diving in the Maldives or hiking to Machu Picchu in Peru. They could pretend they were somewhere far away from Chatelaine— and all the real-life worries and problems that meant their time together was limited.

He unzipped his duffel bag to drop his keys and wallet inside. "We've got sodas, water, beer and a couple bottles of wine. So, let me know when—"

Her tie-dyed T-shirt sailed over his shoulder to land on the bed, and he forgot what he'd been about to say. He spun to see her in a little red bikini top and pair of denim cutoffs that were low enough to show her belly button. He'd seen her completely bare and beautiful, but this bikini with its string ties was even better than finding her topless. He let go of his keys without taking his eyes off her and heard them hit the floor. Just like he was hoping her shorts might do.

Her lips puckered in a way that he'd learned meant she was trying not to laugh. The sassy little tease knew exactly what she was doing to him. And he was enjoying it very much.

"Can we drive around the lake for a while?" she asked. "Maybe stop and swim somewhere?"

"You got it."

He reminded himself that boating and swimming *was* the reason he'd planned this mini adventure. Not for the use of the bed. They had two of those back at the motel that they could use any time. This trip was about more than that. He'd planned it because he enjoyed spending time with her, and their talks and the laughter always left him smiling. He pulled his own shirt over his head and stole a few kisses before they went up on deck, where she continued her deliciously slow seduction.

"Will you put this sunscreen on my back, please?"

She held out a tube of cream. "And then I'll put some on you."

"It's a good thing you didn't ask me to do this while we were down in the cabin, because I would've been hard pressed not to pull that little string and untie your bikini top."

"Hmm," she purred. "I'll have to remember that."

They spent some time cruising around and exploring all the areas of Lake Chatelaine. They saw people waterskiing and fishing and enjoying the sunny day. When they were almost back to the cove where they would dock later, he slowed the boat. "How does this spot look for swimming?"

She came up behind him at the wheel and wrapped her arms around his waist. "Looks perfect to me."

"Excellent. I could go for a cold drink, too." He turned in her arms. "And a kiss."

"I can help you with one of those things right away." She eagerly proved her point.

As another boat drove by, he heard catcalls and whistles. He broke their kiss to see a group of college-age guys craning their necks to look at Morgana. He couldn't exactly blame them. He waited to see if she'd say anything about it, but she was so focused on him, she didn't even seem to have noticed. His chest warmed with her attention. She made him feel…special.

He dropped the anchor but turned around in time to see Morgana shimmying down her denim shorts.

"Catch me if you can, Mr. Fortune!" She jumped into the water with a whoop of excitement. When she resurfaced, the look of joy on her face made him chuckle. She was smart and mature with a good head on her shoulders, and even though she had a serious side, she had retained a youthful playfulness that he found so appealing.

She's irresistible.

His heart was in the danger zone, and he knew it, but that was a problem for another day. Today was too good to taint with worries he couldn't do anything about right now.

He tossed in the lounge floats, grabbed two cans of ice-cold beer and jumped in after her. She climbed up on the yellow float and flipped her long hair over the back to trail in the water behind her. Her bright red bikini was slowly driving him wild.

He stuck a can in the cupholder of each float and climbed onto the blue one. Hand in hand so they wouldn't drift apart, they floated near the boat and talked, sharing childhood stories. After they were tired and hungry from swimming, they lounged on the deck and snacked on fruit and cheese.

Morgana rolled onto her stomach to sun her back and propped herself up on her elbows. "Have you ever been on one of those giant private yachts?"

"A couple of times. Is that something you want to do?"

"I've never really thought about it," she admitted. "I've mostly thought about the locations I want to visit but not the mode of transportation."

He could easily imagine showing her the world,

but that was something you did when you were in a relationship.

Maybe it doesn't have to be.

He *had* made it clear that he never planned to marry again. Maybe they could meet somewhere in the middle? He'd previously jumped to the conclusion that she wouldn't want a friends-with-benefits agreement, but she could make up her own mind about whether or not she wanted to get together now and then with an understanding that it would not become a forever thing. Future get togethers would be a lot of fun. It wouldn't hurt to talk to her about the idea. On another day.

He tucked her hair behind her ear. "Speaking of traveling, I have to take a business trip to Houston. I'll be gone for three days."

"For the big new business deal that you're working on?"

"Yes. Hopefully this will tie up some of the loose ends."

When the sun started to slip close to the horizon, he drove them back to the private dock. They watched the sunset from the deck and ate a delicious picnic meal he'd talked his cousin Bea into preparing for them. The wine with dinner was good, but Morgana's company was so much better.

"Bear, thank you for planning this day for us. It's been wonderful."

"Thank you for being so fun and easy to be with." He idly played with her long, tapered fingers, and she hooked her leg over his as they lay side by side on the deck. The night sky was clear and perfect for stargazing. He knew almost nothing about astronomy, but Morgana did and pointed out some of the major constellations.

When they saw a shooting star, he made a wish. The kind that was rarely granted, because having it all was a huge ask.

For two days, Bear had been out of town on business, and Morgana missed him way more than she ought to. She couldn't stop thinking about him. How it felt to be in his arms kissing him. Sharing secrets. And the way his deep laugh surrounded her like a warm blanket.

"Why did I fall for him, setting myself up for the torture of missing him once he's gone for good?" she whispered.

She put away her housekeeping cart and headed toward the lobby for a cup of midday coffee. She'd been craving the crème brûlée flavored creamer she added to the small coffee, tea and snack bar she'd set up and been put in charge of. Moving around the few pieces of furniture, she'd made space in a corner of the small lobby, and it had been a hit with the guests.

Hal was reading a fishing magazine when she went into the lobby and gave him a list of maintenance issues that needed to be addressed. "Good afternoon."

"Morgana, I know you've been looking for extra

ways to earn money, and I might have something for you."

"Great. What is it?" Even though her car was being taken care of, she could always use extra money in her savings for whatever situation popped up next. Pumpkin would need to be replaced at some point.

"It's really late notice, but the LC Club is looking for extra staff for a big fancy party. It would be a good chunk of extra cash."

She propped her arms on the counter. "That sounds like a good opportunity. Do you know what I would be doing?"

"Tidying up, removing glasses and hors d'oeuvre plates, and general bussing duties."

An upside-down feeling twisted her stomach. Not long ago, she'd sat in the fancy establishment eating and drinking fine wine at a secluded table with a gorgeous millionaire bachelor—who fully intended to remain single. He would also be leaving all too soon. Being spoiled by him would end. So, she would take this temporary job and get back to being the one who cleaned up after other people while they enjoyed themselves and celebrated.

Their dinner date at the LC Club had been a Cinderella moment, and she needed to remember that she lived in the real world. And she needed the money. "When is the party?"

"Tomorrow night. It's for Freya Fortune's birthday party."

Morgana gasped. That was July 25—the same date as her grandmother Gwenyth's birthday!

"Something wrong?" Hal asked.

"No. Not at all. Just excited to make some extra money." At least Bear was out of town and wouldn't be there to see her bussing tables while his family celebrated. "Can I have the number of the person doing the hiring?"

"Sure thing." He wrote the manager's number on a sticky note and handed it over. "I told them what a great employee you are. You'll have no trouble getting the job."

"Thanks, Hal." She rushed back outside without getting the cup of coffee she'd gone in for. Her brain was hyped up enough just thinking about what the date of Freya's party could mean. "July 25. What are the chances?"

It was possible that Freya's birthday was earlier in the week or several days from now and the party was only on the twenty-fifth because it was a Saturday and convenient, but the coincidence… This was another huge clue that gave credence to her growing suspicion.

Is Freya really Gwenyth Wells?

Could the woman who dodged her at every turn be her grandmother? A woman who was so secretive and honestly, kind of sad and lonely. She should just walk up to Freya the next time she saw her and ask if she was really Gwenyth Wells. *Because if you are, you're my grandmother.*

She just might do it because enough was enough!

* * *

Because her car needed so much work and they needed to order parts, Morgana didn't have it back yet, so Hal gave her a ride to the LC Club. He offered to come back and get her if she couldn't find a ride home after the event. She couldn't ask for a better boss.

The fancy party for Freya Fortune's birthday would be starting soon. None of the guests had arrived, but the host, Wendell, was there to make sure everything was ready. Morgana was arranging appetizer plates and silverware when she noticed him standing alone in one corner just observing the setup.

She made her way over to him. "Hi, Wendell. You certainly throw a nice party."

He shrugged. "Thank you, but all I did was write a check."

"Well, it's a very nice thing to do for your brother's widow. Is today her actual birthday?"

He thought for a minute. "She said her birthday was in July, and when I asked her when a good time for a party would be, she picked this date. But I'm not actually sure if it's her real birthday today or not."

Why was it so damn difficult to find out the truth? "I read the unopened letter from Ariella," she blurted out and then wished she hadn't. She shouldn't have brought up this topic right before the party started. She didn't want to ruin his night of fun.

Wendell took a deep breath. "Tell me."

She hesitated. "Maybe now isn't the time to talk about it—"

"I knew it. It's not good news." He wiped a trembling hand across his brow. "I can't wait another second. Just tell me."

She pulled out two chairs at the nearby table and motioned for him to sit. "The date of the letter was the same day of the disaster."

"I received it a day after that."

"Ariella wrote that she left her baby with a sitter for the night because she was going into the mine to get her boyfriend so they could elope."

"But if they'd both run off to elope, he wouldn't have been in… Oh." His eyes filled with tears as realization hit. "My daughter was the fifty-first miner."

She covered his wrinkled hand that was resting on the table. "Yes, I believe so. I'm so sorry."

His next breath came out shaky. "I remember something of hers was found in the mine after the collapse. I just figured it was her beau who'd had it."

"She also wrote that she would contact you at a later date to see if you wanted to meet your granddaughter."

"The baby." Wendell wiped his eyes. "Did Ariella say who was looking after the baby?"

"I'm afraid not." Morgana saw the catering manager watching them. "I'm sorry, but I should get back to work before I get fired. Are you okay? I won't leave you if you aren't."

"I'll be fine. You go do what you need to and don't worry about me. Your concern for me means a lot."

She stood and smoothed her white blouse. "We can talk more tomorrow or anytime you want to."

"Thank you, Morgana. Your family must be proud that you're such a kind and caring young lady."

His compliment made her feel good, but it also made her a little sad that she didn't have anyone except her mom to be proud of her. What a colorful family history the Fortunes had. What a family history she had herself. Maybe Bear was right to be disillusioned about the past.

Morgana went back to work but now she was upset for Wendell as well as grumpy about the whole Freya situation, and in general just feeling down in the dumps because Bear would soon be leaving for good. She just wanted to confront Freya and find out the truth once and for all, but she couldn't do it tonight. Just because she'd gotten in her head about her short romance coming to an end and was generally having a bad day, she didn't want to spoil the elderly woman's big night.

Chapter Twelve

Bear hadn't thought his business in Houston would be finished by today, but they'd come to an agreement, signed contracts, and he'd made it back to Chatelaine in enough time to put on a suit and leave for Freya's birthday party at the LC Club. He'd knocked on Morgana's door as soon as he'd returned to the motel, but she hadn't been there. When he'd called her to see if she wanted to go with him to the party, she didn't answer, and he'd only been able to leave a voice mail. It worried him that he couldn't get ahold of her, but he reminded himself that he wouldn't always be around to look after her, and she was a capable woman.

While he'd been away, he thought about Morgana's suggestion to get a 411 Me DNA kit like Esme had and decided he'd do it. He'd already bought a kit and sent it off. If he got no results from sending in his DNA, and still wanted to take it further, he could hire someone to investigate. But he'd take it one step at a time.

Arriving at the LC Club reminded him of that first dinner with Morgana, and looking out over Chatelaine

Lake brought to mind their boating adventure. The memories of their days and nights, their long talks and making love were something he'd have forever. He still hadn't talked to her about the idea of getting together several times a year because he was still debating whether it was a good idea or possibly the worst he'd ever had.

I'm being as decisive as a hormonal teenager.

The club's ballroom was filled with Fortunes of all ages. He liked seeing his brothers so happy. West was such a good father, and currently had a baby in each arm. Camden was dancing with the woman he loved while big band music played, and people were talking and laughing, but his mind was so far away from it all, the chatter faded into the background. He'd only been here a few minutes and already wanted to leave. Finding Morgana and spending what little time he had left in town with her was all he wanted to do. Preferably back at the motel, where they could be alone to talk and start saying their goodbyes. Now, he just wanted to get this event over with and see if his dancing queen was home.

And that was the problem.

His consuming desire for her was a sign that he'd let himself get too close. Too vulnerable. But he'd be gone soon, and after a period of adjustment, he'd be fine. Until then, there was no harm in enjoying what little time they had left. They'd made lots of memories, and he could reminisce about his sweet, sassy Morgana whenever he wanted. He'd hold dear their days and nights together and suspected she would as well.

Two of his cousins, brothers Damon and Max Fortune Maloney approached, both of them laughing about something.

"Didn't I see you drinking scotch on the rocks at our last get together?" Max said and handed him a short glass with a large, perfectly round ice ball surrounded by amber liquid.

"Yes, you did. Thanks."

"You looked like you could use a drink." Damon held up his cocktail in the universal sign for cheers.

"Am I that obvious?" Bear chuckled and took a sip. It was top-shelf scotch with a smooth, smoky flavor.

"The last time we were all together here at the LC Club was the big New Year's party our oldest brother Linc threw," Damon said.

Max swirled the ice in his drink. "It was an over-the-top splashy way to reveal he'd become a millionaire."

Bear had been somewhere on the other side of the world that New Year's Eve. "I've heard some talk about that party. Isn't that when your family started getting your money one person at a time from Wendell?"

"Yes, and I had to wait until last," Damon said.

The two brothers turned to their mother as she approached and started having a whispered conversation. All he heard was something about their sister and stopped listening.

One of the little redheaded boys that had been wearing a superhero cape the other day skidded to a stop in front of him with a cupcake in each hand. "You're the bear, right?"

He chuckled. "My name is Bear. It's short for Barrington."

"I'm Benjy Keeling Fortune Maloney. Look what I got." He held up one chocolate and one vanilla cupcake. "But Mama said I can only eat one."

The kid was cute and renewed his desire to become a dad. "Which one are you going to eat?"

Benjy licked frosting from first the vanilla and then the chocolate. Some of the colorful sprinkles fell into the front pocket of his white dress shirt. "I like the chocolate one." He held out the vanilla cupcake that was missing a sizable dollop of frosting on one side. "Want this one?"

"No thanks. I already had mine." He was trying so hard not to laugh.

Benjy shrugged. "That's okay. My little brother Jacob will eat it. Bye," he called over his shoulder as he dashed away.

Damon turned from the conversation with his mom and came closer to Bear. "That was our little sugar monster. He's the oldest."

"Cute kid. You must've been really young when you had him."

"My wife, Sari, already had the two boys when I met her. But I adopted them once we got married, and then we had our baby girl." He smiled at his wife a few tables away. She was a lovely woman with long red hair like her boys, and she was holding their baby.

"You have a beautiful family."

"Thanks. I have to agree with you. I'm a lucky man."

Bear supposed some people could be lucky in love and make it work. He just didn't happen to be one of them. Sipping his cocktail, he scanned the room and his stomach fluttered when he saw Morgana on the other side of the ballroom. He was so happy to see that she'd been invited. But why was she holding a stack of dirty dishes? That's when he paid more attention to what she was wearing. A slim black skirt and white blouse with a black tie. It was a caterer's uniform.

She looked in his direction, and he started to raise his hand to wave, but she swiftly left the room.

No wonder she hadn't been at the motel. She was working at the party, and if he wasn't mistaken, avoiding him. But why?

With a stack of dirty dishes teetering in her grasp, Morgana dashed through a doorway at the back of the ballroom that led to the kitchen.

What is he doing here?

He was supposed to be out of town working on a business deal that would make him even richer. Had he told her he wouldn't be home tonight because he didn't want to bring her as a date to a family party? Suddenly lightheaded, she paused to get her bearings.

That was an unpleasant thought. She didn't want to believe that he was embarrassed of her.

She had spotted Bear right before he saw her, and she hoped her pretense of not seeing him was convincing enough that he didn't know she was avoiding him.

Why am *I avoiding him?*

That was a question she should seriously consider. Seeing him here at the party when she hadn't expected to had thrown her off kilter, and she wasn't exactly sure what was wrong with her. True, she'd been a little down and grumpy all evening, but she'd never been ashamed about making an honest living.

She stowed the dishes where they could be washed and started refilling trays with hors d'oeuvres. Morgana wished she could just leave, but she had a job to do.

After their night on the boat, she fallen even harder for a man who could never be hers. And since he'd left for Houston, she'd discovered what it was going to be like to miss him. It was a reality check she didn't care for.

Seeing Bear amongst all the other finely dressed partygoers had stirred up a swirl of conflicting feelings. She wanted to run across the room, leap onto him and kiss him silly, but she also wanted to hide. And hiding was the cowardly emotion that had won out in the end. It was ridiculous. She cleaned his room all the time, but something about him being in a designer suit at a big fancy party and her toting around dirty dishes really highlighted the differences in their lives.

It wasn't like anyone was treating her poorly. Haley and some of the other women had chatted with her, and everyone was kind, but she felt so removed from the Fortunes all dressed in their finest with their great wealth on display. Most of all Bear.

Their futures looked nothing alike. He was a filthy rich bachelor who planned to remain that way, and even though they both wanted to be parents, she would not start a family without being married to a committed partner with mutual love binding them. She could not let herself settle for less and didn't see how she could make that happen when their futures looked so different. And sadly, she predicted Barrington Fortune would end up miserable if he kept his heart on lockdown.

She tended to some of the duties in the back so she wouldn't have to see Bear, but she couldn't stay in the kitchen all night. At some point she'd have to face her fears and feelings. And a little thing called reality.

She gave herself a pep talk the way her mom would do. There was nothing wrong or embarrassing about what she was doing. She was working and making ends meet. When she went back out into the ballroom with fresh trays, Bear was waiting for her right inside the door to the ballroom.

"Hello, beautiful."

She couldn't help but return his big smile. He had sought her out, proving he wasn't completely avoiding her. He looked so handsome in a charcoal suit, the pink shirt she loved and a silver tie. "Hi, yourself. I didn't know you were back in town yet." She held out the tray, and he took a bacon-wrapped pepper on a toothpick.

"I just got back. I only had enough time to knock on your door and then get dressed before coming to the party." He popped the bite-size hors d'oeuvre into his mouth and followed her as she took the trays to a long table set up along one side of the ballroom.

"You knocked on my door?"

"I did. I wanted to see you."

She shoved down the giddy feeling his words caused. He might've wanted to see her, but he had not said he'd planned to invite her to be his date to this party. Experiencing this very public employee and guest dynamic between them was something she couldn't ignore.

A stark reminder that what they had was not some real and lasting love story.

The fact was Bear was leaving soon, and he didn't want any kind of committed relationship. He was planning to pay a surrogate to carry his heir, for goodness' sake. If the option existed to use nothing more than a test tube, he'd likely do it because it would completely remove the risk of getting attached to the mother of his child.

"I should get back to work. I need to go get more trays of food and clear some dishes."

"Of course. Sorry. I shouldn't be keeping you." He

swayed forward like he'd kiss her but only squeezed her hand and then stepped away. "Come find me when you get a break."

"Okay. I'll try." She once again fled for the safety of the kitchen.

Why did I start sleeping with him?

She sighed. Oh, yeah. Because she'd thought it was a grand idea to experience everything life had to offer and have a no-strings-attached love affair. Talk about living and learning the hard way. There was no chance of them ever ending up together. She'd been deceiving herself in a big way to even hope, and a fool to think she could sleep with him and not fall in love.

But for him...

I'm nothing more than a fling for Barrington Fortune.

More food was served, and dishes cleared. Morgana's feet were aching and so was her back as she watched people dancing and drinking and Bear laughing with his brothers.

Freya was standing alone, and it was the perfect opportunity to ask if this was her real birthday. She was almost certain that she'd put enough clues together to suggest that the elderly but vibrant woman standing beside an ice sculpture was her grandmother. Besides the age range and birthdate, there were little things she'd said and done over the months. She'd known that the bookstore was once a hardware store, and it's true someone could've given her that information, but the way she'd said it was as if it were first-hand knowledge. And then there was the major clue about her revealing to West and Tabitha that she had a daughter with whom she'd been long estranged.

She only had to walk up to her and ask, but she also had to tread carefully because she didn't want to ruin her special night.

Freya looked so elegant in a long champagne-colored dress with a gauzy shawl collar. Her ash-blond hair was in a fancy twist on the back of her head. She was observing her party with an odd expression that wasn't exactly joyful or melancholy but something in between that was tender and touching. She held up her left hand and gazed at her diamond ring. Who was she thinking of? Her late husband?

Morgana approached her with a smile. "Happy birthday, Mrs. Fortune. You look beautiful."

"Thank you. This is such a lovely party. But it makes me miss… Elias." Her words had trailed off to a whisper.

That must be why she looked so wistful. She really had loved Elias Fortune.

Morgana's chest tightened, and she frowned as hope faded. Loving Elias would suggest that Freya was not Gwenyth. Her grandmother never would have married the enemy. But she had to be sure.

"Is today your actual birthday?"

Freya stiffened ever so slightly, but it was enough for Morgana to know she'd struck a nerve.

"Excuse me, please. I'm needed over there," the old woman said and hurried away.

Way to just throw it out there with no finesse.

Now Morgana was even more confused. Why dodge her question if she wasn't Gwenyth? She sighed. This was not helping her frustration level. She'd walk right out the front door if she didn't have to work.

When she entered the kitchen, the manager waved her over. Her heart plummeted. Was she about to get in trouble? She shouldn't have been chatting with the guests. As if she needed another reminder of her place.

"Morgana, it's your turn for a break. Thanks again for filling in tonight on such short notice. Hal was right about you. You're a hard worker who also takes the time to make people feel welcome."

"Oh, wow. That's so nice to hear. Thank you."

"Take thirty minutes off your feet. There will be lots of work to do once the guests leave." Something clattered in the kitchen and the manager rolled her eyes with a sigh and went to investigate.

Morgana headed back toward the ballroom. Bear had told her to come find him if she had a break. Had he truly meant it? "Guess I'll find out."

She made a quick stop in the bathroom to check her appearance. All she could do was smooth her ponytail and add a dash of mint lip gloss from the tube in her pocket, and then she went back out into the ballroom. It only took a few seconds to spot Bear standing with his brothers, and she started walking their way but hesitated. Was this wise?

He saw her and excused himself from his family to head her way. "Hey, there. How's it going?"

"I'm on my break."

He held out his hand. "Excellent. Come join us."

She looked down at herself, feeling self-conscious in her server's uniform. "I'm not really dressed for the occasion. I was thinking I'd just go outside or something."

"My lovely dancing queen, don't you know you're the most beautiful woman in the room?"

"There you go again with your master-level flirting."

He chuckled. "You bring it out in me, sweetheart. Don't you want to dance with me?"

"I do, but…" She adjusted the collar of her white blouse.

He held up a finger. "Give me one minute. Will you meet me by that door to the balcony?"

"I'll be there." She smiled, her tension beginning to melt away. She made her way through the thinning crowd and waited where he'd indicated. He returned shortly after with a bottle of champagne, two glasses, and over his arm was a beautiful red silk shawl she'd seen Haley wearing. She opened the door, and they went out onto the balcony.

"Why do you have Haley's shawl?"

"She let me borrow it." He put the bottle and glasses on the ledge of a planter, and then like her fairy godfather, he wrapped the silk around her shoulders and loosely tied it. "Red is your color. It makes me think of your little red bikini."

Butterflies were skyrocketing around her insides. She suddenly felt like Cinderella at the ball. Just like in the fairy tale, the clock was ticking, but she was going to make the most of every second. "You think I should wear more red?"

"Definitely." He gently pulled the hair tie from her ponytail, and with his hand on the back of her head, he fluffed her hair.

She closed her eyes and moaned as delicious tingles spread over her scalp. "You have a magic touch."

His warm breath fanned across her cheek as he whispered in her ear. "I'm just getting started, sweetheart."

She slid her arms around his waist and met his gaze. "Why are you doing this?"

"Because you deserve it. And I like to see you smile." He moved them into a slow dance to the muted music from the party. "Most beautiful woman at the ball."

"With the most handsome man." She rested her head on his chest and inhaled his clean and spicy scent.

They danced until the band took a break and then stood at the railing sipping champagne and looking at the lovely view. The night was breezy, and the water softly lapped against the shoreline. She jumped when a firework exploded in a shower of silver sparkles that rained down over the lake. It was quickly followed by another, the colors reflecting on the water.

"Did you do this?"

He chuckled and kissed her softly. "I wish I'd thought of it, but no."

"I wonder what the occasion is?"

In her fairy tale retelling of this Cinderella moment, the fireworks would be just for them. If only she had a glass slipper to leave behind.

Chapter Thirteen

Bear was leaning against his car outside of the LC Club while he waited for Morgana to finish working. Their time together on the balcony had been wonderful but far too brief, and he hated watching her go back to work when he knew she was tired. She'd told him that Hal gave her a ride out to the LC Club and another waiter was giving her a ride back to the motel because he lived nearby. That had made him instantly jealous, which was ridiculous.

Very soon it would be time for him to leave Chatelaine. Back to his regular nomadic lifestyle, which suddenly felt tiresome and a little depressing. Moving from fancy hotels and rented condos was getting exhausting. After watching his family members setting down roots in homes that they owned, he knew he needed to start thinking about doing the same.

Along with finding an egg donor, buying a house was a necessary step that had to be completed by the time a surrogate was carrying his baby. The big question was, where in the world to settle?

The back door to the LC Club's kitchen opened

and he straightened, hoping it was Morgana, but it was only two young women who laughed and talked as they walked to a little black car. Once again, he wondered who the guy was giving her a ride. Was it someone closer to her age who wasn't jaded like him? Another flash of jealousy hit him. "Dammit. What the hell is wrong with me?"

His tie suddenly seemed to be choking him. He yanked it loose and walked another lap around his car, the fine gravel crunching under his Gucci shoes. At the heart of it, they were from very different worlds.

He was glad he hadn't yet brought up the topic of being friends who get together for special benefits several times a year. The jealousy curling through him proved *he* was the one who couldn't handle an arrangement like that with Morgana.

For a little while longer they could enjoy the short amount of time they had left together. He'd talk to her about it tonight. They could take their time saying goodbye. Then that would be the end of it. They'd be left with great memories.

This time the feeling in the pit of his stomach wasn't the flashfire burn of jealousy. It was…panic. And it was totally unacceptable.

Being here was a mistake. He needed to leave, but right when he opened his car door, Morgana came out the back door with a tall blond who looked like he was the star quarterback type. The kind of guy who had no trouble with the girls.

"Bear." Her smile blossomed—for him. Not the other guy. "What are you still doing here?"

He went around and opened the passenger-side door and tried to get his heart rate under control. *Get it together, dude.* "We're going to the same place, and I thought I could give you a ride."

She turned to the young man beside her. "Thanks so much for the offer of a ride, but I've got it covered."

"Maybe another time," he said and looked bummed as he walked away.

Bear couldn't blame the guy.

"Thanks for waiting for me," she said and came close enough for a kiss.

He pressed his lips to hers and savored the moment of connection. His anxiety started to melt away and he felt control returning.

On the drive back to the motel, she told him about her conversations with Wendell before the party and how sad he'd been. Now, finding out what happened to Ariella's baby was on the list of mysteries to solve.

She adjusted her seat belt. "When I got to the LC Club tonight, I was almost certain all the clues plus the date of the party meant that Freya was really Gwenyth."

"Now you don't?"

"I spoke to her toward the end of the night. But right before, I watched her staring longingly at her wedding ring. And then she talked about missing Elias, and it was obvious she had loved him." Morgana's tone turned pensive "So, I don't see how she could be Gwenyth. My grandmother was so set on vengeance against the Fortune brothers that there is no way she would've fallen in love with and married one of them."

"What about the birth date?"

She sighed. "She dodged that question, as usual. Another loose end that I can't seem to tie up."

He swung his car into his usual spot at the motel. "Your room or mine?"

She smiled and nibbled on her full lower lip in the seductive way that she had learned drove him wild. "Mine. I want to take a quick shower after working all evening."

"You can take a shower in mine. *With me*," he said with a big grin and leaned across the console to kiss her.

"Do you have shampoo that smells like flowers?"

He chuckled. "Nope. I do not."

"Then I guess you'll just have to join me in my shower."

"I'd love to take you up on that offer, sweetheart."

They walked up to her room, hand in hand and started kissing the moment the door was closed behind them.

Tomorrow would be soon enough to talk to her about him leaving Chatelaine. Tonight was too special to tarnish with talk of their imminent goodbye.

Morgana's whole body was taking flight. The evening that had started out so crummy had turned into the kind of beautiful night she'd remember forever. She loved it when Bear kissed the spot right below her ear and then went on a slow and gentle exploration that made her shiver from head to toe.

"Too many buttons," he muttered as he worked on the top one on her blouse.

She giggled. "You have just as many."

He grabbed the lapels of his shirt like he was going to rip it open and send buttons flying across the room.

"Barrington Fortune," she said with a gasp. "Don't you dare rip this beautiful pink shirt. It's my favorite."

He growled but then grinned and returned to working on her buttons. "Maybe you better tend to mine."

"Good idea." She took his suggestion and ran with it all the way down to his belt buckle. Their arms were tangled, and they were laughing so hard it took twice as long as it should have.

He finally shrugged off his shirt and tossed it on her desk. "You can keep my shirt."

They left a trail of clothes from the doorway to the small bathroom.

There was an extra level of tenderness in Bear's touch. More intensity in his kisses. Something about tonight felt different. A little more special.

Before Morgana had even opened her eyes the next morning, she was smiling. Bear's chest was warm against her back and his arm was stretched out along her leg with his fingers splayed on her thigh. It made her feel so...calm and cared for. Like everything would be okay.

They'd made love late into the night, but she was on such a high from their romantic evening that she was wide awake. It felt like they'd jumped a level in their relationship, and she'd almost told him she loved him, but caught herself just in time. It was way too soon for that. Especially knowing how skittish he was about relationships.

They might not be planning a future together, but would he still claim what they had wasn't a relationship? How could he deny it at this point?

His deep, even breaths told her he was still sleeping, but she had a few ideas about how to wake him up. First, savoring the present moment was most important. It was so nice to feel safe and protected and... in love.

Oh, God, I'm so in love with Bear Fortune.

But was Bear in love with her, or just really good at seduction? She'd swear that she felt something new in his touch. A stronger connection.

The time on the bedside clock caught her eye, and she remembered she had to start work early this morning.

Nooo. Why today?

All she wanted to do was lounge in bed like they'd done the day they watched the 1980s movie marathon, but she had a commitment. Sighing, she slipped out from under the covers without waking Bear, and hurried into the bathroom to get ready for work.

He woke when she leaned down to kiss him good-bye. "Where are you going?" he asked in a sleepy, gravelly voice.

"Unfortunately, I have to start work early this morning."

"What time is it?"

"Seven."

He grasped her hand and tugged her down to sit beside him and then rested his head on her thigh. "What do you have to do so early on a Sunday morning?"

"For one, the other maid, Rhonda, is out of town and it's just me today. You know that big group who is here for a family reunion? They paid extra for breakfast, and I have to get it set up in the lobby." The large group had taken up the eleven rooms that weren't occupied by her, Bear and Freya.

"You have to cook?"

"No. It's only pastries, fruit, yogurt and little quiches made in muffin tins. I just have to warm them." The tiny kitchen tucked away at the back of the lobby wasn't the easiest place to do anything, but it had been her idea to offer a breakfast option for an additional charge. At the moment, she was thoroughly annoyed with her entrepreneurial ideas.

"Hurry back so I can have you for breakfast." He hiked up the skirt of her uniform and kissed her knee.

Something about the action was so tender that it threatened to make her cry. She needed to get out of here before she told him that even though she'd said she wouldn't, she'd fallen head over heels in love with him.

"I plan to clean your room last so you can be my reward."

He sat up. "Good plan."

"I started my coffee pot for you and you're welcome to anything in the refrigerator." She kissed him once more and then went to find her shoes. "It will be a few hours before I get back. When the big group leaves, which will thankfully be earlier than usual, I have to clean their rooms for another group who is coming for some event at the lake and are due for an early check-in."

He sat up and the sheet pooled in his lap, and the muscles of his chest and arms flexed as he stretched. It was enough to make her want to quit her job and climb back into bed with him.

"I have work to do as well. I have to prepare for a ten o'clock meeting."

"Where do you have to go for it?"

"It's virtual," Bear told her. "I'll just be in my room on the computer."

"I'll make sure not to interrupt. See you in a while." She blew him a kiss from the doorway.

"See you soon, sweetheart."

A few steps away from her room, Morgana glanced around to see if there was anyone who could see her, but deciding she didn't care who witnessed her happiness, she danced all the way to the office. The feelings coursing through her were like nothing she'd ever experienced. She felt light and floaty like she might drift up into a castle in the sky, but at the same time, powerful and grounded in a way that made her feel connected to the universe.

The day was too good to ruin with any thoughts of the Freya drama. It could wait until tomorrow.

She hummed and sang quietly while prepping breakfast and then taking care of the guests. As soon as they finished eating and checked out, she got to work on their rooms. When she was on the last of their rooms, she looked at her watch. At Freya's request, she had a set schedule for cleaning her suite— mostly so the old woman could avoid her. If she went right now, she'd be early. She'd started the morning with the mindset of not wanting to think about the elderly woman, but now, she wanted it done and over with.

She would ask Freya outright if she was Gwenyth Wells and if she still refused to answer, she would tell her she was Renee's daughter and see if that got a reaction. It had waited long enough. Whether she was or wasn't her long-lost grandmother, at least she'd know one way or the other. Then she could concentrate on a path to the future she hoped to have with Bear.

She knocked on Freya's door, waited and then knocked again, but there was no answer. She used her key, and like always, called out once more before stepping all the way into the suite.

It was quiet and dark, except for the glow of the screen saver on Freya's laptop.

Morgana flipped on the lights and kneeled to pet the orange cat who'd hopped off the bed to greet her. "Hello, Sunset. Have you been a good boy?"

The cat purred and arched into her hand for a back rub.

On today's cleaning schedule, Freya's room was not due for a deep cleaning, but it wouldn't hurt to take her time in hopes the woman would return. But not too long because she was eager to see Bear.

The first time she'd met him, he had told her he'd be leaving town when his business deal was done, and from what she'd heard him say on a few work-related phone calls, she had the impression he would only be here another week or so. She had to make the most of it.

It was wholly unwise, but she was holding out hope that in the time they had left, she could make Bear see that he didn't need a surrogate to have a baby. She wasn't like his ex-wife and would never tromp on his heart the way she had done with his best friend. That he could have love in his life again. *With her.* Because loving him and having his child had moved to the top of her list of hopes and dreams.

Morgana went into the bathroom to gather the towels, and when she came out, she once again noticed that Freya's laptop screen was up. She stepped forward and then back and then forward again, battling with herself about what to do. Curiosity won and she sat down at the desk. There was no way she could get lucky enough that it wasn't password protected,

but it wouldn't hurt to check. With a deep breath—
and a quick prayer to forgive her for this breach of
privacy—she clicked a key. The screen came to life,
with no need of a password.

She gasped because she hadn't expected it to work,
and guilt hit her, but she couldn't take her eyes off
the screen. It was open to an unsent draft email. It
looked like Freya was writing a letter to someone.
When Morgana saw the intended recipient, her heart
skipped a beat and then took off racing.

Chapter Fourteen

Morgana pressed a hand to her stomach and the other one over her mouth and stared at the letter on Freya's computer screen. It started with the words Darling E.

"Could E be Elias? What is going on?" Was Freya writing it as catharsis even though Elias was dead? She refocused on the letter.

Darling E,
When I fell in love with a man named George Jessup, things started to change in my life. It was your love that helped me set aside my vendetta against Edgar and Elias Fortune for what they did to my family.

A whoosh of goosebumps spread across every inch of her skin, and she squeezed her eyes closed and tried not to get her hopes up too high. Considering the number of people who died in the mine, it was highly possible someone else also wanted vengeance against the Fortune brothers. But what were the chances? She kept reading.

Then when you went to the hospital, imagine my shock when I discovered your true identity. I was furious and felt betrayed even though you knew me as Judy Jones, an alias I created when I started my search for the Fortune brothers. But at the time, I was too blinded by emotions. I'd fallen in love with and married one of the very men I'd been hunting for vengeance against my first husband, Clinton Wells.

"No freaking way! It's been true all along. Freya Fortune is my long-lost grandmother, Gwenyth Wells. I knew it." Morgana shot to her feet but immediately sat back down to keep reading, too curious about what else she might discover.

That's right, I'm the mine foreman's widow who un-knowingly married Elias Fortune. Once I discovered your true identity, I came to Chatelaine to restart my efforts for revenge. I took your will that said you were leaving everything to your and Edgar's grandchildren, and I told them all that at your request, I'd grant each of them their most fervent wishes—only to destroy them.

"Haley was right. She's been behind all of it."

Now, I am so ashamed of myself and so sorry for what I did when I first arrived in town. I sabotaged their lives, but then everyone was surprised and so happy when they discovered West wasn't really dead. It was then that I knew for sure that I had to stop. I realized that I truly cared about all of the Fortune grandchildren.

It's terribly tragic that I didn't learn my lesson the first time. Because of my obsession with vengeance, I lost my own daughter, Renee, to estrangement when she was eighteen. I've looked for her over and over, but I've never been able to find her.

I'm so sorry that I lied to your grandchildren about your death. I'm still holding out hope, my darling, that you will come out of the coma and be able to read this letter.

"Oh. My. God. Bear's grandfather, Elias Fortune, is still alive? This is huge news."

Freya's email was so emotional, and it was clear she truly loved Elias. When Morgana tasted salt on her lips, she realized she was crying.

The lock clicked, the door opened, and Freya froze in place. Morgana was still sitting at her computer, wiping tears from her eyes. It was pretty clear that she'd invaded this woman's privacy, read the email and knew everything.

"I... Oh my." Freya burst into tears and ran away.

Morgana jumped up, tripped over the cat but caught herself before completely going down. Once she'd righted herself, she ran out the door after her. She now had the proof that Freya was Gwenyth, and she needed to tell her that she was her granddaughter. Her car was still here, but no matter where she looked, there was no sign of the woman who had apparently gone by three different names at different times in her life. Gwenyth Wells, Judy Jones and Freya Fortune.

Morgana leaned forward with her hands on her

knees. The spike of adrenaline was waning and making her nauseous. She abandoned her search and went upstairs to find Bear. She peeked through the crack in the curtains to see that he was not on his computer so she knocked and then opened the door.

He turned from the tiny closet, and the smile immediately fell from his face. "What happened? Why are you crying?"

She sat on his bed beside the suitcase he was unpacking from his recent trip. "Freya is really Gwenyth Wells. I have proof."

He kneeled in front of her and took her hands in his. "Did you talk to her? What did she say?

She shook her head. "She ran off before I could tell her that I'm her granddaughter."

He pushed the half-empty suitcase aside, sat beside her and pulled her onto his lap. "Start from the beginning and tell me everything."

"Freya… I mean Gwenyth, came in and saw me reading a letter she'd written." From the comfort of his arms, she told him her grandmother had sabotaged the very wishes she'd been granting, and also that she'd looked for her daughter, Renee.

"Wow. You hit the payload of information."

"I really did. I have to tell my mom about this, but I'd really like to talk to Gwenyth first, so I have some idea of what to tell her."

"I'm sure she'll be happy no matter how you say it, sweetheart."

"Bear, I haven't told you the part that is going to

shock you the most. Your grandfather, Elias Fortune, is alive."

His eyes widened almost comically. "For real?"

"That's what the letter said. She hopes he will come out of his coma and be able to read her letter."

"We should go look for her." His jaw hardened and she felt his arms tense around her. "She has some explaining to do. We need to see if she'll come clean."

"Now that I've read what she wrote and she ran away in tears, I don't know how she can deny it."

They left his room and started their search. When they had no luck, he finally called Freya, and she answered.

"Hello, Bear." She sniffed as if she was crying.

"Freya, where are you?"

"I needed to take a walk."

He put the phone on speaker so she could hear. "I'm with Morgana, and we're looking for you."

"Oh. Oh my. I guess you know everything?"

"I doubt I know everything, but I do know we'd like to talk to you, please."

She sighed. "Okay. Can you please help me call all of the Fortunes together so I can tell everyone the truth all at once? I hate the thought of repeating it over and over, but I will if it's necessary."

"I don't think there's any reason for that," Bear said. "This is a lot to explain. I'll call everyone, set up a meeting for tonight and then get back to you with the place and time. You're not going to skip out on us, are you?"

"No. I'll be wherever you tell me to be. As of right now, I'm done with doing the wrong thing."

A few hours later, Bear's brothers, cousins, their families, and Wendell and Morgana were all gathered together at the Cowgirl Café. Since it was closed on Sunday nights, they had the place to themselves. Plus, the advantage of having drinks and snacks readily available.

He could tell Morgana was nervous, so he put an arm around her shoulders and gave her a light squeeze as the last couple of people took their seats.

"What's all this about?" West asked and grabbed a nacho from one of the plates in the center of the long stretch of tables they'd pushed together.

Freya stood from her chair at one end of the table. "I have some things I need to tell everyone. I need to confess."

"This should be good," someone mumbled, and then someone else shushed them.

"When I met your grandfather, Elias, he was using a different name. I knew him as George Jessup. And he knew me by my alias, Judy Jones. It was completely unexpected, but we fell in love and got married."

"Hold up," Haley said. "You got married without even knowing each other's real names?"

"I understand that it's hard to believe, but it's true. It wasn't until I saw his last will and testament that I realized I'd married Elias Fortune. The very man I'd been hunting."

"Hunting?" several voices asked in unison, and then everyone started talking at once.

Bear stood and held up his hands in the universal sign for everyone to quiet down. "Let her finish. You're all going to want to hear this. Trust me."

Freya wrung her hands and waited for everyone to settle and give her their attention. "I was so angry and hurt when I discovered the truth of who I'd married that I acted without giving it enough thought." She took a shuddering breath and scanned the group, meeting everyone's gazes as if she wanted each of them to know she was talking directly to them. "My shameful plan was to grant your dreams and then destroy them, but it all unraveled because I grew to care about all of you so much."

Bear glanced up and down the table at the stunned faces. Everything from the wide eyes and slack jaws you would expect to see, plus a few others like the salsa dripping off a chip that was halfway to Asa's mouth.

"I was the volunteer who saw a nurse switch the babies and that's why I gave Esme the DNA kit, so she'd find out fast."

Esme sucked in a quick breath, then hugged the baby boy in her arms and reached over to take the tiny hand of the baby on her husband's lap. The two babies born on the same stormy night who were not related but were now being raised as brothers. The one Esme had brought home from the hospital and fallen in love with and the one who was her biological son who was being raised by a widowed father. The man who was now her husband.

"Esme, I am more sorry than you'll ever know," Freya choked out. "I don't expect you to ever forgive me, but I am truly sorry for the pain I put you through. I wish with all of my heart that I could go back in time and make better choices."

Esme leaned against her husband, Ryder, and kissed the top of the baby's head who was sitting in his lap. "Complete forgiveness might take some time, but…if you hadn't done it, I wouldn't be married to a man I love dearly, and I wouldn't have two adorable sons to love."

Freya then went on to spill the rest of her transgressions. She admitted to Asa that she had exaggerated his sowing his wild oats so the owner of the ranch wouldn't sell to him unless he was married. Then she confessed to Bea that she'd caused the mishaps on opening night of Cowgirl Café. The very place they were sitting in that had thankfully become so popular. Freya also divulged she had originally created red tape for Camden's horse camp, but quickly undid that because she couldn't bear to keep children from doing something so special.

"When West returned from the dead, I found myself so happy for him and all of you that I stopped my shameful vendetta." Freya steepled her pointer fingers and pressed them momentarily to her lips. "And because I have grown to truly care about all of you so much over the months. I completely understand if none of you ever wants to see me again." She sat down as if every bit of her strength had left her in a rush.

Morgana pushed a glass of ice water her way. "Have a drink."

"Thank you, dear."

Everyone was oddly quiet as they processed the wealth of information they'd just been given.

"I forgive you," Wendell said. "I can identify with making poor decisions and wishing you could change things you've said and done."

Bear's cousin Asa put an arm around his wife, Lily. "You know, you actually granted more wishes than you think. If you hadn't done what you did, I wouldn't be married to this amazing woman. You led us to love, and I'm willing to forgive you."

"Thank you." Freya wiped a tear that slid down the soft skin of her papery cheek. "But you might want to hold that thought until I finish telling you everything."

"There's more?" Camden gritted out.

Bear and Morgana shared a knowing look, and she laced her fingers with his under the table.

Freya took one more sip of water, and then cleared her throat. "Elias is alive."

Now, no one was quiet. Everyone was talking at once and getting louder.

She held up her hands and tried to shush them.

"Let her talk. I want to hear this," Wendell said loudly enough that everyone immediately quieted.

"Elias is in a coma at a private hospice care facility on the Texas Gulf Coast. In Galveston."

There was another moment of stunned silence before Bear steered the conversation to the information Morgana most wanted to hear. "You've only gone by the name Freya since you came here?" he asked.

"Yes. That's right. I became Freya Fortune when I arrived in Chatelaine."

"No wonder you didn't always answer the first time someone called your name," Wendell said.

"What do we call you?" Bear's brother Camden asked. "Freya Fortune, Judy Jones or… What was the other one?"

"Gwenyth Wells," Morgana said.

The elderly woman pressed her fingertips to her lips as if to hold in emotions. "I haven't gone by the name Gwenyth in so many years. But I would like to be that person again. I liked her so much better than the bitter woman I've become."

Morgana squeezed Bear's hand and then stood. "Can I say something?"

"Why not," West said. "What else could there possibly be that would surprise any of us?"

Bear snorted. "With this family? Hold on to your cowboy hats, boys and girls." He winked at Morgana and mouthed, "You've got this, dancing queen."

Chapter Fifteen

Bear's support meant so much to her and gave her that little extra bump of courage and calmness she needed to continue. "You all know me as Morgana Mills, but that's not my real name."

"*Another* secret identity?" Bea asked.

"My name is Morgana Wells." From the corner of her eye, she caught several confused expressions, but she focused on the woman she'd been seeking for months. "I'm the daughter of Renee Wells."

"Oh, my goodness. You're my granddaughter." Freya clasped her hands to her mouth, and once again, everyone was stunned by the news and talking at once.

Morgana put a hand on Freya's shoulder when she swayed in her chair. "It's okay. Take a breath."

Tears welled and began streaming down Freya's cheeks. With trembling hands on the table, she pushed herself to stand and pulled Morgana in close. "I'm so sorry, sweetie. I should have known. I've been so blinded by my need for revenge, and I've been so horrible."

Morgana hugged her back, and her own cheeks were wet and her heart full. "I found you. It'll be okay."

Bear stayed close to them while still giving them a moment of privacy, and everyone else was up and talking in whispers with animated movements.

Her grandmother put both hands on Morgana's cheeks. "How could I not know? My beautiful granddaughter."

"I guess I should've said something sooner. I just wanted to be sure."

"I'm so glad you came looking for me, and so sorry that I made it so hard for you. Looking back, now I understand why you were asking so many questions. I'm glad you didn't give up on this stubborn old woman." Freya pressed a hand to her chest. "Does your mother know you've been looking for me?"

"No. I didn't want to get her hopes up until I knew for sure." Morgana looked at her watch. "I'll call her tomorrow."

"Tell me everything. Where have you been all these years that I couldn't find you?"

"I grew up on a big communal farm in rural Tennessee. That's probably why you couldn't find us." Morgana caught Bear watching her from across the room and returned his smile.

Her grandmother followed her gaze. "You really like him, don't you?"

"I really do." Her stomach filled with butterflies. *Heaven help me, but I'm so in love with that man.*

"Tell me more about growing up on a farm."

"It was a good life, but I did have to work hard."

She smiled softly. "Now I know that's a good thing because I know the value of a hard day's work."

"Were you born in Tennessee?" Freya asked.

"I was. We have a doctor who lives on the farm, and I was born at home."

"Renee always was drawn to a simple life. I hope she's been happy."

"She has. She loves working in the orchard and with the animals." Morgana sat with her grandmother for a while longer and gave her a brief overview of the last twenty-five years in Tennessee.

Some of the Fortunes approached the two of them and told Freya that they would be happy to welcome her into the family—even though they'll be keeping a watchful eye. Freya said she couldn't blame them, and their welcome was more than she deserved. Esme and Bea asked to talk to Freya privately and offered to give her a ride back to the motel.

Before Freya left with them, she hugged her granddaughter one more time. "Can we spend time together soon?"

"I'd love that." Her cheeks were starting to ache from smiling. "I'll see you tomorrow."

"I'm looking forward to it, dear."

As she watched her walk away with Esme and Bea, Morgana began to think about the best way to reveal such big news to her mom. Should it be over the phone or video chat, or should she go home and tell her in person? No, it would take too long to travel back to Tennessee, and Freya… *Gwenyth* was too excited for it to take that long.

It was getting late, so they all moved outside and began to say their goodbyes. While Bear was talking to his brothers in the parking lot of Cowgirl Café, Morgana caught up to Wendell before he could get into his car.

"Wendell, do you have a second to talk?"

He stopped and turned to her. "Certainly. Do you have another juicy secret?"

"No, but I do have a thought I'd like to run by you." Over Wendell's shoulder, she caught sight of Bear hugging each of his brothers. "What if the two notes about the fifty-first miner have been left by Ariella's child? Maybe she discovered her identity and is searching like I've been doing."

He shook his head and rubbed the back of his neck. "That's a good thought but it's impossible."

"How can you be so sure?" Bear's arm slid around her waist, and she leaned into him.

"Because I know who it is. It was me," Wendell said.

Shocked to the core, Morgana put a hand on the elderly man's arm. "*You* left the notes? Why?"

"I did it hoping someone would investigate and find out what became of Ariella. I've been too afraid to delve into it, afraid to discover that my daughter perished in the mine instead of running off with the baby." His eyes welled with tears. "And now that I know that is exactly what happened, I want to find my granddaughter."

"I think that's a wonderful idea," she said.

"I should've said something inside while we were all gathered together, but there was so much else being revealed that I thought I should wait. Once things settle down a bit, I'll look for my granddaughter, just like you looked for your grandmother and found her."

"Why wait?" Bear said. "Now that we have more information, I think it's time to hire a private investigator."

"You know what? You're a smart young man." Wendell slapped Bear on the back good naturedly. "I'm going to go hire one right now."

The old man hugged Morgana and whispered, "Don't let time slip away like I did. Share what's in your heart."

As Wendell walked away, she reached for Bear's hand, and he laced their fingers. His touch sent comfort spiraling through her.

"It's been a big day," Bear said.

"It certainly has, and now I'm exhausted."

"Let's head back to the motel." He kissed the top of her head and they moved toward his car.

Bear had been clear from the start. He did not want a serious relationship. Never planned to marry again. And he wasn't interested in love. At least those were the words he'd said, but she had begun to suspect he was only trying to convince himself, because the way he was with her told a different story. One where there were feelings deeper than two people just hanging out like she'd originally suggested.

She gazed at him. Bear was the most romantic man she'd ever known. A delicious combination of masculine, thoughtful and tender. Was Wendell right? Should she tell Bear that she'd fallen in love with him? "How are you feeling about everything that happened today?" she asked him cautiously.

"Me? I'm fine. I never knew my grandfather but hearing that he's still alive is a good thing. It's you I'm concerned about."

"I'm good. Happy but emotionally exhausted."

"I bet. You've been busy. We know who Freya really is and all the other secrets because you kept after it and found the answers you were looking for. Do you need to call your mom in Tennessee and give her the news?"

"I do, but I'm so wound up right now that I need to calm down first and get my thoughts in order." She sighed. "You'd think by now I would've planned out exactly how to tell her I found her mother, but I'm not sure. I just want it to be perfect."

"Want to come back to my room and I'll give you a back rub to help you relax?"

She leaned into him. "That's an offer I can't resist."

But in truth, it was *him* she couldn't resist. Maybe Wendell was right. She should just go for it and tell Bear what was in her heart.

In his room, Bear sat on the end of the bed and pulled off his boots while she remained standing.

Morgana's decision to tell him what was in her

heart had given her a burst of energy. "I have one more thing to tell you."

"It couldn't be more surprising than some of the things we've learned today. Lay it on me, sweetheart." He stood and came over to her.

She put her arms around his neck and liked the way he cradled her hips and pulled her closer. "I know that relationships or any talk of love scares you."

"I don't think *scared* is the right word. It's more like caution."

"Cautious can be good, but… I guess it's all the coming clean and secrets being revealed that have given me the courage, so I'm going to go with it." She let her fingers trail up into his hair. "I'm in love with you."

He stiffened and dropped his arms. "Morgana—"

"Bear. Let me finish while I still have the courage. I want to have your baby, but not just to give our child to you and only be a part of their life. I want to be the mother of your child…and your wife. We can be a real family where everyone loves everyone." The expression on his face made her warm cozy feelings flash freeze into blocks of ice around her heart.

"Sweetheart." He shook his head and crossed the small room. "You don't understand. You're young and haven't been through what I have." He grabbed a stack of jeans from a drawer and then dropped them into the open suitcase.

The sudden chill increased to encompass the air in her lungs. Why was he putting things *into* his suitcase? Maybe he just wasn't thinking about what he was doing. "Are you packing or unpacking?"

"I'm packing."

"Another business trip so soon?"

He came back over to her and took both of her hands in his. "It's time for me to leave Chatelaine."

"And me." Her voice quivered and her whole body went painfully numb and empty. "For good? You're leaving because I love you?"

He closed his eyes and rested his forehead against hers. "You've always known my time here was temporary. You know I don't do serious relationships."

She pulled her hands free from his hold and turned to the window. That was so much crap! The man was lying to himself.

"I'm sorry, Morgana. This is exactly what I didn't want to happen. I never wanted you to get hurt."

"I understand." She didn't understand it at all, but she suddenly felt so defeated and empty. She knew there was nothing she could say to make him love her.

"I wish it could be different."

With her throat and eyes burning, she swallowed back the pain and tears and spun to face him. "Thank you for fixing my car and for…everything." She opened the door and stepped out. "Goodbye, Bear."

Fleeing from his room was difficult, but running from the heartbreak was going to be infinitely harder.

Chapter Sixteen

Bear had broken his own rule. He'd hurt Morgana, and it was torture.

He glanced in his rearview mirror long enough to see the Chatelaine Motel growing smaller and smaller until it was gone from view. His stomach was twisted in knots, his head throbbed, and his heart felt like it was being squeezed by a vise grip. He was leaving behind a part of himself, but there was no other choice.

If he turned around and went back to her and then truly lost Morgana at some point, it would crush him even more than it had when his marriage ended.

Where had he gone wrong? Had he not been clear enough when he told her about his rules and plans, or was Morgana just more naive than he'd thought?

The drive to Houston went by in a blur, and now Bear sat in the dark living room of his furnished rental condo with a glass of scotch in his hand and heaviness on his heart. The city skyline at night was impressive and made him think of watching fireworks with Morgana on the balcony at the lake. He wished he could share this view with her, because without her… It was unimpressive and only reminded him that there were people out there who were living their lives. Loving spouses and children and building homes to share with their families.

He tipped back his crystal glass and drained every last drop.

Bear knew he couldn't be what she needed. He was older and jaded and too broken for someone as sweet and as innocent as Morgana. She was young and full of big dreams and sparkling butterflies. At some point, one of them would end up broken. There was no reason to set yourself up for that kind of pain.

Morgana had been curled up in bed ever since Bear left the night before. She'd called and told Hal she was sick and couldn't work. It might not be true in the normal sense, but she was heartsick. Her stomach hurt, her head hurt, and she was humiliated and berating herself for being so foolish. He'd been clear about what he did and didn't want, and she should've listened. But still…

She had filled with a love like she'd never known only to be crushed under the weight of the walls around Bear's heart. He was apparently right about her being naive. She was embarrassed that she'd been so gullible.

Their ending hadn't been as tragic as him catching his wife with his best friend, but heartbreak was still so much more painful than she'd known it could be.

Finally knowing what real romantic love was and losing it so rapidly was enough to give a girl whiplash.

Bear had taught her what it was to be in love with someone, and just as quickly, he'd taught her about heartache.

She'd been so wound up and excited after the family meeting that she'd put off calling her mom, and now she was too emotionally crushed for the big reveal. Her mom would instantly know there was something wrong, and it would ruin the big surprise she'd been working on for months. Morgana wanted the conversation to be nothing but joyful when she told her she'd found Gwenyth. And right now, she was anything but that.

A knock on her door startled Morgana, and she clutched the pillow closer to her chest.

Could it be Bear? Did he come back?

For a few more seconds she let herself hope that he'd returned to sweep her off her feet, but she knew her fairy tale was over, and she couldn't bring herself to move. Because if she crawled out from under the covers, she'd have to face the real world. She just couldn't. Not yet. She wanted to lose herself in sleep and not have to feel the searing ache of not having her love returned. Morgana didn't intend to let her pity party go on for long— she just needed a few more hours to lick her wounds.

The knock sounded again.

What if it really is him?

She threw back the covers and went to the door

to make sure, but one glance through the peephole killed her hopes.

"Morgana, are you in there? It's Haley."

With her foolish hopes dashed, she opened her door and did her best to keep her lips from trembling.

Her friend studied her face. "Oh no. This won't do."

"What won't?"

"I was afraid of this," Haley said. "You've been crying. Can I come in?"

"Sure." She turned away but left the door wide open for the other woman to come inside.

Haley flipped on the light and then sat in the desk chair. "It's true? Bear left Chatelaine?"

"He's gone."

"It's not just another business trip?"

Her throat burned as she held back tears. "No. He's gone for good. He's moved on with his life, and I'm not in it." Morgana sat on her bed and then flopped onto her back to stare at the ceiling. "I fell in love, and he didn't."

Haley sighed. "I'm so sorry."

Morgana told the other woman everything that had happened between her and Bear. Well, *almost* everything. Some of the memories were precious and only for her.

"I've seen you two together and the way Bear looks at you…" Haley came over to sit beside her and reached down to give her shoulder a comforting squeeze. "The man loves you. I think he just can't admit it. Give it some time. His family lives here, and he'll be back to visit them."

Morgana shook her head. She knew that before this trip Bear had been out of touch with his family for months, and he'd likely do it again. "I'm not so sure about that. He's pretty set on not having any kind of serious relationship with a woman, and clear about what he wants out of life. A wife is not on his list, but having a husband *is* on mine."

"I'm glad you are smart enough to know yourself and what you want long term."

Emotionally exhausted from the conversation, Morgana abruptly changed the subject. "Have you found out anything more about the possibility of you having a fourth sibling?"

"Not yet, but though none of us can wrap our brain around the possibility, my sisters and I are still going to look into the rumor that we're actually quadruplets and have a brother," Haley said.

"Please let me know if I can help in any way."

There was another knock on her door, and she caught her breath again before she could stop herself. She had to stop torturing herself with false hope. Barrington Fortune wasn't coming back to her this time. She answered the door to see her grandmother.

Freya's bright smile turned into a frown. "Are you alright, honey?"

The way she said it reminded her so much of her mom, Renee, that she lost the small amount of control she had over the tremble in her lips and tears spilled from her eyes as Morgana motioned for her to come inside.

"I didn't realize you had company. Hi, Haley," Freya said.

Haley stood. "I'm going to get going and let you two talk. Morgana, call me. Anytime."

"I will. Thank you for coming to check on me."

When the door closed behind her friend, her grandmother sat on the bed and patted the spot beside her. "Come tell me what's going on. Is your mom upset to hear that you found me?"

"No. I haven't called her yet. I'm so sorry. I know you're anxious but…" Her voice choked up as she took a seat.

"It's Bear, isn't it?"

She nodded with her lips pressed tightly. "It didn't work out."

She repeated some of the things she'd just told Haley, and they talked for a couple of hours.

Freya told her own stories of heartache and shared the hard-earned wisdom of where she went wrong and how she would do things differently if she could.

Getting advice was a bit of a comfort, and Morgana now had some perspective. "I think I'll take a shower, so I look presentable before I have a video chat with Mom."

"That's a good idea. I'll be in my room if you need me. And just like Haley said, you can call or come to me anytime. Day or night."

"Thanks, Grams."

MAKENNA LEE   189

The old woman's eyes lit up. "Oh, I like that name. I can't tell you how wonderful it is to hear it."

It was also nice to be able to say it. Morgana was feeling a little bit stronger and was once again excited to call her mom.

Morgana got in the shower and had one more cry about Bear before washing her hair. Once she was dressed in her favorite sundress, she put on some makeup to conceal her dark circles and red-rimmed eyes. Then she got comfy on her bed and dialed her mom's number for a video call.

"Hello, honey. How is your adventure going?" Renee's big sun hat shaded her face as she walked through the pasture where the dairy cows grazed.

"It's going good." Small lie, but as far as their family went, it was nothing. "I have several things to tell you. First, I'm in Chatelaine, Texas."

Renee stopped walking. "Why? Are you just that curious about where I used to live?"

"I was definitely curious, but there's more. I found your mother," she said in a rush.

It took a lot to shock her supercalm and down-to-earth mom, but Morgana had done it. Renee Wells stood motionless with her mouth attempting to say words, but nothing was coming out. She took a few steps back then sucked in a startled breath.

Morgana caught a glimpse of her mom falling butt-first into the water trough before the phone sailed through the air to land with a view of the sky through the branches of her favorite climbing tree.

"Mom! Are you okay?" Morgana started to laugh and sprang up off the bed as if she could do anything from halfway across the country. But then her stomach plummeted when she heard what sounded like crying. "Mom," she yelled, not even knowing if she could hear her. Then the sound became very familiar laughter, and her tension eased.

Renee picked up the phone, her hat gone and her curly hair wet and clinging to her cheeks as they both continued laughing. "Well, that certainly cooled me off. I can't believe I fell in the water trough, but I thought you said you found my mother."

"Maybe you should sit back down, but this time not in the water."

Her mom leaned her back against the tree instead. "Are you trying to tell me that really is what you said? You found Gwenyth?"

"Yes. I found her. I met my grandmother, and she's been looking for you for years."

Renee wiped her cheeks, and this time it wasn't because of water from her unexpected dip in the cattle trough. "Really? I can't believe you found her. Is that what you've been doing this whole time?"

"Yes. Don't be mad."

"I'm not mad, honey."

"Thank goodness. It took me a while, and you won't believe all the twists and turns I ran into along the way."

She told her mom all the details of her search. The

ups and the downs and all the unexpected secrets that were revealed along the way.

"I'm so glad you're willing to get together with your mother. Do you want to come here or for us to come home to Tennessee?"

"Maybe we should start with a phone call and see where it goes from there," Renee said softly.

"Sounds like a good plan, Mom." She smiled. "I'm going to give you her number so you can call her."

Once Morgana hung up the phone, she realized how hungry she was. In a little while she would go down to her grandmother's room, check up on how their conversation went and see if she wanted to go out for something to eat. Because if she continued to mope and crawl under the covers in her room, she'd cry herself to sleep all over again.

After a long workout in the condo's fancy gym and then a shower, Bear pulled a T-shirt over his head and caught the lavender scent of the laundry soap Morgana used at the motel. He held the collar to his nose, inhaling as memories came at him hard and fast. Missing her wasn't going to be as simple to get over as he'd told himself it would. He tugged on a pair of jeans and felt a lump of fabric near his knee.

"What is that?" He shook his leg until whatever it was fell out the bottom and landed beside his foot. He bent to pick it up, and his throat tightened. It was one of Morgana's glass slipper socks.

It must have gotten mixed up with his stuff the

last time she'd done his laundry, even though he'd always told her she didn't have to. He held it to his chest for a moment, then feeling silly about being so emotional, he folded it before putting it in a drawer with his own socks.

"This feeling really sucks," he mumbled as he went to the bar area of the condo. He'd told himself he wouldn't try to drown his sorrows with a drink, but that was a goal for tomorrow.

Ice clinked in the Swarovski crystal glass as Bear took a sip of scotch, the burn of it sliding down his throat, mimicking the way his heart felt. It was ridiculously expensive and his favorite, but it tasted like dirt in his mouth. He drained it in one quick gulp and then shuddered.

After forcing himself to do some work on his newest project, he realized it was the middle of the night, but he still couldn't sleep. He leaned back on the uncomfortable black leather sofa that was positioned to look out over the Houston skyline. The furnished condo his assistant had rented was a penthouse. It was modern, sleek, minimalist and quiet as a tomb. Bear had once craved this kind of order and solitude. But now?

There was no one singing or laughing or gently brushing his cheek. No kid's toys scattered about like they were at West's house. No love. He felt...empty. Completely empty. It was a physical pain in his chest. He missed his brothers and the twins and his whole extended family. But most of all, he missed Morgana. He missed her more than he'd ever missed anyone.

He grabbed the remote control and turned on the huge television that was mounted on one wall. An old episode of *The Golden Girls* was something he would normally never watch, but at the moment he didn't care. He just needed the droning noise of it to fill up some of the emptiness.

He would only be in Houston for a month while he tied up loose ends with his new business deal, so he really didn't need this large two-bedroom place. It seemed so over the top and unnecessary. He'd grown used to his cheap motel room, and he ached with every fiber of his being for the woman two doors down. A hollowness in the pit of his stomach left him feeling unsteady.

"Morgana, my dancing queen, what did you do to me?"

The next morning, Bear sat at the kitchen breakfast bar with a cup of strong coffee and scrolled through his email, scanning for anything that needed his immediate attention. He paused on one from 411 Me DNA.

"It's my DNA results. That sure was quick."

He opened the email and stared at the information. Along with 50 percent of his heritage coming from Mexico, there was also Italy, Wales, Scotland and Sweden. He also had DNA matches. None were parents or siblings, but he had lots of distant cousins, a couple of first cousins and one aunt.

As he stared at the information he'd been looking forward to, and at the same time dreading, he wasn't sure how to feel. There was an option to send a message to DNA matches, but he brushed it off. He had enough information.

And frankly, since he'd left Morgana, there wasn't much he cared about, including the new work project he'd normally be pumped to start. He'd lost his desire to take off for a foreign country, and he had no appetite.

He tossed his cold untouched toast into the garbage. This level of emotional response wasn't normal for him. "This has got to stop."

Bear poured a fresh cup of coffee and took a seat on one of the stools at the breakfast bar. With work pulled up on his laptop, he tried to fall into the rhythm that usually came so easily, but thoughts of Morgana and his family in Chatelaine kept flashing in his mind. He'd left town so abruptly that he hadn't even been able to say goodbye to everyone in person.

Two cups of coffee later, he changed his mind about contacting his birth family. For the first time ever, he knew for certain that he had blood relatives, and the curiosity was nagging at him. There was possibly someone with all the answers to a lifetime of questions. Mainly, why was he abandoned?

He closed the work document that he couldn't focus on and typed a message to his aunt. He told her he was adopted as a toddler and was curious about his birth family and asked her to contact him. Once he sent off the email, he went for a long run, hoping the physical exertion would exhaust him enough to be hungry and to get some sleep, so he wouldn't stress over whether his aunt would get back to him or not.

Fortunately, he didn't have to wait long. That evening, he received a phone call from an unknown number, but he answered right away.

"Hello. This is Barrington Fortune."

"Hi, Barrington. This is your aunt Rita."

His pulse picked up speed. "Thank you for getting back to me, and please, call me Bear."

"Bear. That is so fitting. I love it. I'm sure you have a ton of questions for me."

"I do." He walked to the huge windows overlooking the city. "First, what was my birth name?"

"Seth Sanchez."

Hearing his birth name for the first time was a surreal mixture of unknown and déjà vu. "Are my parents living?"

Her sigh was soft, but he heard it, and he knew the answer before she said it. "They both died many years ago. Your father, Carlos, in a construction accident shortly after you were born, and your mother, Silvia, died of cancer a few months after you went to live with the Fortunes."

His throat burned as he pressed the heel of one hand against his chest. "She knew she had cancer when she…left me in the park?"

"Yes. That's exactly why she did it. Her cancer was terminal, and she didn't know what else to do. We were very poor and lived with my grandmother who was seventy-five and not in the best health herself. I was only fourteen years old, and your mother was nineteen."

"Why didn't she contact the state or put me up for adoption?"

"Your mama and I were in the foster system for a little while before my grandmother took us in. We didn't have a good experience, and she didn't want that for you." There was a long pause. "I wanted to keep you *so badly*, but I was too young, and my grandmother was too old, and we had no other family. I was already grieving the sister I knew I would lose way too soon and letting you go was the hardest thing any of us ever did."

He heard her sniff in a way that suggested she was crying. "I imagine it felt like an impossible situation."

"It really was. We all loved you so very much. Giving you up broke our hearts more than you can imagine. When your mom discovered she had cancer, she couldn't see any other way. She was sick and desperate to find a better life for the son she adored."

He had imagined all kinds of scenarios for why he was abandoned, but this act of desperation hadn't been one of them. "Why did you say the name Bear was fitting for me?"

"Two of your favorite things were bears and digging in the dirt. On the day Mrs. Fortune found you,

you were wearing a blue shirt with a cartoon bear on it and holding your favorite stuffed bear. It was also one of the words you knew how to say. Is that why they gave you your name?"

He shook his head. "I have no idea. I always thought it was because my little brothers had trouble saying Barrington, but I do remember having a black bear with a blue bow tie."

"That's the one. Your dad bought it for you."

He was pretty sure he still had it in a box somewhere in storage, but he didn't admit that to her. "How did my mother decide where to leave me?"

"We scouted around and found a park that was always filled with nice families. It was in a really nice area of town where rich people came with their kids. She put you in the sandbox, which was your favorite place to play. Because as I said, you loved to dig in the dirt as if you were searching for something."

"I still do. I'm in the oil business."

She laughed. It was a musical tone that made him smile. "That is also so fitting."

"I invented some drilling equipment."

"Oh, Bear. Your parents would be so proud of you. I know I am."

"Tell me more about the day she took me to the park," he rasped and sat on the edge of the sofa.

"We hid in a wooded area that bordered the park and watched to make sure nothing bad happened to you. Only a few minutes later, a mom with a toddler about your age came over to play in the sandbox. When she realized you were alone, she picked you up and held you, comforting you while she waited for the authorities. I was young, so I don't know all the details, but somehow, my sister found out where the other mom lived. Silvia was tiny and before she got too sick, she would dress as a young boy and walk our dog past the Fortune's house so she could make sure you were okay. Until she just didn't have the physical strength any longer."

Bear swallowed a lump in his throat. "I can see how that would be impossibly hard on her. Hard on all of you."

"It really was. Silvia made us swear to keep quiet and let you be adopted by a family who could give you so much more than we could. It broke all of our hearts," Rita confessed. "A few years after that, I almost ended up in foster care myself when my grandmother died, but I turned eighteen a month later. I went into the navy and then became a lawyer when I got out. I work with the foster care system, trying to make sure children don't fall through the cracks."

"That's wonderful. I'm sure…" It still felt so weird to call Silvia his mom. "Your sister would be proud of you for dedicating your life to such a worthy cause."

"Are you married or have any kids yourself?" she asked.

"No. It's just me." A flash of pain made him grimace, but he shoved it down in a way he'd become a pro at doing. "And you…?"

"I'm married with two daughters, and we live in Vermont."

It was all so achingly sad yet sweet, and he realized his cheeks were damp. He didn't even know when he'd started crying. "I really appreciate you telling me everything."

"Bear, never again think you weren't wanted. We all three cried an ocean of tears missing you."

"Will you tell me more about my parents?"

"Of course."

They talked for nearly an hour, and he found out all kinds of details about his parents, Carlos and Silvia Sanchez. They made plans to get together in person just as soon as he could get to Vermont. The second he hung up, he wanted to tell Morgana everything he'd learned about his origin. He might've been abandoned, but he was loved and wanted in a way he'd never imagined.

He ached to talk to his sweet dancing queen. To see her. To hold her. And it was 100 percent his fault that he couldn't.

Chapter Seventeen

At his family's request, Bear drove an hour and a half from Houston to Galveston to meet Freya, Wendell, his brothers, and his three cousins, Asa, Esme and Bea. He was the first to arrive at the private hospice facility where Elias had been for months. It was a huge two-story home that had probably been built in the early 1900s and had been immaculately restored.

Even though he was in a coma, Freya wanted everyone to be there all together at least once. Bear wasn't fit company for anyone but hadn't been able to deny her. His brothers and Wendell were the next to arrive. He raised a hand in greeting and walked toward them as they got out of the car. He so badly wanted to ask about Morgana, but he bit down hard on the inside of his cheek instead.

"Are you doing alright?" West asked as he studied Bear's face.

He tried to harden his features to hide the vulnerability that had crept in. "I'm fine."

Camden snorted and shook his head. "Someone's a liar, and his britches are going to catch on fire."

"I have to agree with your brothers." Wendell squeezed Bear's shoulder in a grip that felt weaker than only days ago. "You look a bit worse for wear compared to how you did back home, young man."

The word *home* made Bear wince, and he knew they saw it. "It's a small adjustment period. No big deal." But he was starting to seriously doubt his own words.

"Weren't you the one who gave me the advice not to let fear of getting burned again keep me from the woman I love?" Camden said.

Bear shrugged. "That's what I thought you needed to hear, not what I expected for myself."

Before they could once again call him a liar, a maroon SUV pulled up and the rest of the group piled out. This time, Bear worked even harder, forcing a mask of cheerfulness to fit his face. Thankfully, his cousins didn't know him as well as his brothers because his state of happiness didn't seem to be in question with them.

"Thanks for meeting us here today," Freya said, but her expression told him she wasn't happy with him, and it wasn't hard to figure out that it was because of the way he'd left. The way he'd broken her granddaughter's heart.

The eight of them went inside the house and crowded into Elias's private room. Other than the medical equipment around his bed, it looked nothing like a hospital. It had plush carpet, expensive furnishings and fine art on the walls.

Freya—who he'd have to start thinking of as

Gwenyth—sat on the edge of her husband's bed, took his hand and kissed his forehead. "I'm here, my love. I brought your brother Wendell and yours and Edgar's six grandchildren."

Wendell sat in the plush armchair closest to the bed but didn't say anything. He looked as if he needed to get his emotions under control first.

Freya told them the sweet story of how they first met and then a funny one about when Elias tried to catch a raccoon that had gotten into the house. It put everyone more at ease with the situation and the atmosphere became more relaxed.

Wendell cleared his throat. "I've been waiting to have all of you together again so I can share the newest development. I'm sure you've all been told by now that I'm the one who wrote the notes about the fifty-first miner."

"So we would look for your daughter," Esme said with a nod.

"Yes." He told them some of what Bear already knew. "I always wondered what happened to my daughter Ariella, and now I know she died in the mine with her baby's father. For way too many years, I was too ashamed of my actions and how I treated her to reveal anything about her. But with all the secrets coming out lately and with the help from some of you, I've located her daughter. I—I have another granddaughter."

"Oh, that's wonderful." Bea said. Everyone else joined in with well wishes and questions.

Bear smiled. One he didn't have to fake. He was happy for his great-uncle because he finally had answers to questions he'd been holding on to for way too long.

Freya gasped, interrupting Wendell's story. "He squeezed my hand!"

They all moved closer as she kept talking to Elias and stroking his cheek. "Please wake up, darling. Everyone is here to see you, and I want so badly to talk to you."

Elias blinked his eyes and groaned. He tried to speak but coughed.

"I'll get a nurse," someone said from behind Bear.

Freya soothed her husband with tender touches. "Don't try to talk yet, my darling."

"Water," he croaked in a voice hoarse with long disuse.

Wendell was closest to the pitcher of water and poured a glass, and then Freya helped Elias take a small sip.

"Sweetheart," Elias whispered and lifted a trembling hand in an attempt to touch her face.

She took his hand in both of hers and lifted it to press his palm to her cheek. "I've missed you so much. I love you."

"Love you. Nice to see…" He struggled for a breath. "Your pretty face."

The door to the room opened. "Mr. Fortune, I'm so glad to see you're awake," a nurse said. "The doctor is on his way. Let me just get a blood pressure reading."

She came around on the opposite side from Freya and started her assessment.

Elias looked around the room full of people and his eyes widened as if he'd only just realized they weren't alone.

"Some of your family has come to see you." Freya started introducing them one at a time. "And your brother Wendell is here, too."

Wendell stood from the chair and took Elias's hand. "Hello, little brother."

"I'm sorry." Elias's voice was still hoarse and gravelly. "So sorry, Wendell."

"Instead of dwelling on the past, let's focus on the future." Wendell swept out his arm to encompass the Fortune six. "Look at all these young people who are here to see you."

"Tell me," Elias coughed and struggled for a breath.

A doctor had come in midway through the introductions and was listening to his heart and lungs, but Elias tried to shoo the man away.

"Just let me do a quick check, Mr. Fortune," the doctor said. "Then you can visit with your family."

"Your lives. Tell me," Elias insisted weakly.

Not knowing what to say about his life, Bear hung back. Everyone talked about the person they loved, their kids, their ranches and homes. He was the only one without a significant other waiting at home. He squeezed his eyes closed and rubbed his forehead.

I'm also the only one without a permanent home.

His rented condo was empty, impersonal and too

cold. But that's the way he'd said he wanted it to be. He'd made his bed, so to speak. When his turn finally came, he stuck to only telling his grandfather about his work in the oil industry.

"Black gold," Elias said with a weak grin

"Let's give them some time alone," Esme suggested once they'd each told him about their lives.

Everyone other than Freya stepped out of the room to give her and Elias a chance to visit. All seven of them settled in a sitting area richly decorated with pricey antiques and artwork. Someone offered them coffee and a variety of homemade cookies. They were the first thing that had tasted good to him since leaving Chatelaine. Since leaving Morgana.

The group talked about West's twins and random other topics, and the whole time he was waiting for someone to mention Morgana, but no one did. The same nurse who'd taken Elias's blood pressure stepped into the room and relayed Freya's request for them to come back.

"I'm afraid it won't be long now," the nurse said softly.

They filed into his room, and Bear's stomach hardened into a knot.

Freya lay stretched out on the bed beside Elias with her hand on his chest. She was crying softly.

They all remained silent, and Wendell sat on the other side of the bed and covered his brother's hand with his own. The only sound was the beeping of medical equipment and a bird singing a mournful tune in a tree outside of the window.

Elias's eyes fluttered open, and he gave his wife a faint smile and whispered something. A moment later, he closed his eyes. For the last time.

The soft beeps from a monitor marked that Elias's heartbeat had begun to slow. When it became a flat line, Bear inhaled a sharp breath that caught painfully in his throat. Just like that, in only a few heartbeats, Freya had lost her partner. There was nothing she could do to stop it from happening. The person she loved was lost to her.

This was one of the reasons he couldn't be with Morgana. He had no choice but to leave Chatelaine. He'd had to make her understand...he couldn't be what she needed.

But why had Freya willingly put herself in this position?

Because she got to be in love, said a voice in his head before he could stop it.

Several people were crying along with Freya, and while he knew they were all glad they'd been here at the end, Bear really needed to get out of here. Seeing Elias and Freya's love for one another and then so quickly watching death come between them was stirring up his own turbulent emotions.

After an appropriate amount of condolences and goodbyes, Bear was getting ready to head back to Houston when Freya followed him toward the front door and stopped him with a hand on his arm.

"Barrington, do you have a minute to talk before you go?"

His skin felt too tight, and he really wanted to get out of here and be alone to sort through his jumble of emotions, but he'd broken her granddaughter's heart, and she deserved to get her licks in.

"Sure. Let's sit over here." He led her to a tiny sitting area near the front door and they sat on the couch. "I'm glad you asked me to come here today, and I'm so sorry about your loss."

She squeezed his hand. "I think Elias woke up because all of you were here. He could hear us talking and laughing about memories. All of you being here gave him the strength of will to wake up for a little while. I'll always be grateful for this last bit of time with him."

"As you should. I'm glad you had a chance for a proper goodbye."

"Whether or not you want to hear it, I'm going to share some of my hard-earned wisdom."

There wasn't much doubt what this was about. Now that Freya knew Morgana was her granddaughter, she'd gone into maternal protection mode and was probably going to give him a scathing lecture about loving and leaving an innocent young woman. He mentally groaned. But he knew deep down he deserved whatever she had to dish out.

"I'm listening."

She took one shuddering inhale. "I've wasted so many years being miserable and seeking revenge when

I should've been enjoying my life and my family. Way too many wasted years that I can never get back."

"I hear you, but I have too much baggage for someone as sweet as Morgana. I need to keep moving."

"You can't outrun your past, Barrington. Trust me on this one. I have years of experience. The heart is always going to be involved." She looked at him with a heartfelt, broken smile. "Don't do what I did. I've seen you and Morgana together. I know she loves you, and if you'll look inside—" she put a hand on his chest, patting lightly over his heart "—I think you'll find that you love her, too."

He was suddenly too choked up to speak.

"Think about what I've said, please. Love is worth everything." Freya pulled a tissue from a box on the side table and then stood. "Be safe on your drive. I'll see you soon. I hope."

Bear turned up the music on the car stereo, but it couldn't drown out the thoughts buzzing like a swarm of bees in his head. What Freya said was true. He was always trying to outrun his past and not get too close to anyone and risk losing them.

But I lost Morgana anyway.

He groaned. "I've gone and fallen completely in love with her."

His feelings for Morgana were not the same as the love he'd felt for his wife, or rather, what he'd *thought* was love. With his dancing queen, it was somehow deeper. Stronger. More complex.

But what about her well-being? I've already hurt her.

Another thought struck him with a harsh slap. If he didn't think he was enough for Morgana, how was he supposed to be what a child needed? If he had a baby using a surrogate, he could hire a whole team of nannies and it wouldn't be enough. Why was he even considering bringing a child into the world who would never have a mother? Why would he want to subject his child to that?

Oh my God. I'm being such an ass. A pigheaded, selfish fool. He realized he was speeding and eased his foot off the accelerator.

"What the hell am I doing?" Bear said to the empty car. "Me leaving Chatelaine hasn't made anyone happier. I walked away from her because I'm scared. She was right. I'm afraid to open my heart."

By the time he got to Houston and stood in the middle of the condo, he knew he had to do something to fix his mistakes. No one was happy with the way things were. Least of all him.

"I love Morgana. I have to get to her and tell her."

Bear's whole body was practically vibrating with a combination of excitement and nerves as he threw clothes haphazardly into a suitcase, not caring what was getting wrinkled or if any of it even matched. Now that he'd made the decision to go after the woman he loved, he couldn't get there fast enough.

The last thing he did before leaving the condo, however, was grab one special item and stuff it into his front pocket.

* * *

Bear parked in his usual spot at the Chatelaine Motel and immediately saw Morgana standing beside one of the new housekeeping carts in front of the downstairs room on the far corner. He wanted to call out to her and have her wave enthusiastically or blow him a kiss. The rush of love for this woman made his heart beat so fast he was short of breath. She was so lost in thought that she hadn't seen him yet, and he watched her for a minute longer.

And he did not like what he saw.

She wasn't singing or dancing or even smiling. Her hands moved sluggishly as if it took all her effort to organize the mini bars of soap and bottles of shampoo.

I did that to her.

Disgust filled him. Hot shame and regret. He'd been the one who crushed her beautiful spirit. The one who made her pretty eyes glaze over with a faraway sadness that tore at him.

He quietly moved closer. "Hi, sweetheart."

She stiffened on a small intake of breath and briefly closed her eyes as if saying a prayer before looking up at him. "You're here."

"I am. Sorry it took me so long."

"What are you doing here?" She wrapped her arms around herself as if she was cold.

"I forgot something."

She clutched the star charm on her necklace. "I

cleaned your room, and I didn't find anything of yours."

"Did you look in *your* room?"

Her eyes filled with hurt as she frowned. "You want your pink shirt back?"

"No." He held out a hand, but she didn't take it. "I'm not here for my shirt. I came back for *you*, sweetheart. I came back for the woman I've fallen head over heels in love with."

She took a step back, and his heart sank. What if it was too late? What if he'd blown his one and only chance? He had bared his truth, and the next move was out of his control. She might very well tell him to take a long hike across a short cliff. Bear had never been so scared.

But then an idea came to him, and he went with it before he overthought it.

Morgana pressed a hand to her chest as if that could slow her hurtling heart rate. Bear Fortune was standing in front of her saying all the right words, and she wanted to fall into his arms, but now she was the one who had her guard up. He'd always said she didn't know heartache, but he'd been the one to teach her that lesson. The hard way.

She'd never seen him this unsure, and when he started backing away from her, she thought he was leaving, but he pulled out his phone. His fingers moved across the screen, and he held his phone above his head like a miniature boom box.

As the song "Dancing Queen" played from Bear's phone, she smiled for the first time and moved a few steps closer. Close enough to touch but she clasped her hands against her tumbling stomach. He was re-enacting a movie scene with a modern twist, and it was so sweet and on-brand for the kindest guy she'd ever known.

"But, Bear, what about the risk to your heart?"

He put his phone in his shirt pocket and caressed her cheek in the most tender move she'd ever seen from him. "My heart is yours, Morgana Wells. I love you, sweetheart. I started falling in love with you the moment I found you standing on my bed singing and dancing, but I was being too..."

"Cautious?"

"Scared. I'm not afraid to admit it anymore. Now, the only thing that frightens me is living the rest of my life without you. I want to sleep beside you every night. I want to make babies with you and build a life together wherever you want to settle down." This time when he held out his hand, she slid her fingers across his palm. "Will you give me another chance to show you how much you mean to me?"

The pressure that had felt like a physical weight on her heart began to lift. With a smile she led him into the empty motel room she'd just cleaned and closed the door behind them. "You want to build a real family together?"

"Yes. More than anything. Completely real in every way possible. A mom and a dad loving one another and sharing the duties of raising children. And I'm not trying to say that you need to have a baby right away. There's no timetable. I just want to start a life with you. Kissing you every morning and every night. Loving you."

She smiled and released the breath she'd been holding since the day he drove away. Morgana stepped into the comfort of his arms and wrapped hers around his neck. "I'd like that very much. I love you, Bear."

He drew her into a deep, achingly sweet kiss and then she buried her face in his neck, breathing in his scent. She wanted to stay this way forever and not risk this being a dream.

"I know it's only been a few days, but I've missed you so much, sweetheart."

"So have I." She tipped up her face to look at him. "But how are you going to kiss me every morning and night when you travel so much for work?"

"I'm glad you asked. I'm hoping you'll want to travel with me, and then when you're ready for children, we'll both stop traveling."

She jumped onto him and wrapped her legs around his waist, loving his strength and how he could hold her this way with no trouble. "That's something else I'd like very much."

"Then, in that case, you should give your notice to Hal. Your cleaning days are over, sweetheart. It's time you had some pampering and a real adventure." He gazed adoringly down at her. "I want to take you to see waterfalls in Brazil and pyramids in Egypt and beaches where you can wear your little red bikini. I'll take you wherever you want to go."

She slid a hand up the back of his neck and into his thick hair, her grin blooming into a smile so big that it made her cheeks ache. "So, you're offering me the world?"

"As much of it as I can give you." His kiss was soft, his tongue barely teasing her lips before easing back to smile at her.

"I can't wait for our first adventure."

He slid a hand low on her back and urged her closer. "Do you know where I want to go first?"

"To bed—I mean the beach?" She giggled and liked the sound of his answering deep laughter.

"I like the way you think. Both excellent options, and that first suggestion is one we should check off the list very soon."

"Agreed. But I'm curious, where is it that you want to go?"

"To a farm in Tennessee where you grew into the woman I love."

Her heart filled with so much love that she felt like she was floating. "You came here to sweep me off my feet, didn't you, Mr. Fortune?"

"Yes, ma'am. I sure did. And speaking of your feet…" He put her on the bed, dropped down to a knee and took one of her shoes off.

"What are you doing?" she asked with a giggle when he tickled the sole of her foot.

He pulled something from his pocket and slipped it

onto her bare foot. When she realized it was her missing Cinderella sock, a lovely shimmer of tingles settled over her whole body. "Look at that. It's a perfect fit."

"Let the adventures begin, my love."

Epilogue

On a cloudy day when the sky itself seemed to know they were sad, the Fortune clan and family friends were gathered at Fortune Castle. Although Morgana's heart was filled to bursting with love, it was a sad day because one member of the family was no longer with them. She straightened the flower arrangements clustered around the eight-by-ten-inch photograph of Wendell.

They'd chosen one that wasn't a stuffy portrait in a suit but rather a candid shot of Wendell smiling at a family barbecue. It suited the loving man he'd become by the end of his life.

Bear slipped his arm around her waist and kissed her cheek. "How are you doing, sweetheart?"

She nestled against his side and breathed in his familiar scent. "I'm alright."

Morgana was so glad that she had talked to Wendell on the phone the day before he passed away peacefully with his granddaughter by his side.

Wendell had left a letter with his lawyer, asking his relatives to hold a celebration of life at his home, Fortune Castle, rather than a somber funeral in a church. He wanted it to be a celebration of Fortunes and of all that the word *Fortune* means.

Once all the guests had gone and it was only the family, they sat in one of the large rooms of Fortune Castle, sharing memories of the unique man who had been in their lives for way too short of a time.

"There's one more thing I want to tell everyone," Bear said. "I've set up a foundation that will make restitution to the families of the miners who were killed in the collapse."

"That's so generous. What a great idea," West's wife Tabitha said.

"We're also dedicating a plaque to my grandfather, mine foreman Clinton Wells," Morgana informed the family.

"That's such a wonderful gesture. I love it," her grandmother said and held a hand to her heart. "Your grandfather would be so proud of you."

"Tell us more about your last conversation on the phone with Wendell and what you've learned about his granddaughter," Haley said. "Not everyone has heard the story yet…"

Morgana snuggled closer to Bear. "Wendell was finally reunited with his long-lost granddaughter, Wendy Windham Fortune, and he died peacefully with her at his side. Wendell also decided to leave her Fortune Castle."

Everyone was full of rapid-fire questions. Where

is Wendy from? Is she married? Does she have children? How did she feel about her grandfather?

Morgana briefly explained what little she knew. "I don't really know very much. Wendy has six adult children, three women and three men. Apparently, they have a complicated past and have decided to claim their family name of Fortune and move to Chatelaine."

"Wow. That's a lot of new family members," Camden remarked. "I'm so curious and can't wait to meet them."

"You'll get that chance sooner than you think," said Eliza, the real estate agent in the family who had married Max Fortune Maloney. "I heard that they bought a huge working cattle ranch in Chatelaine Hills on the far side of the lake."

Asa sat forward to put his drink on a coffee table. "That's a really wealthy area."

"And they'll be moving to town in only a few days," Morgana said.

Bear chuckled. "It's always a wild, unexpected ride with the Fortune family. I can't wait to see what happens next."

* * * * *

Don't miss
Fortune's Secret Marriage
by Jo McNally,

the first installment in the new continuity
The Fortunes of Texas: Fortune's Secret Children.
On sale August 2024, wherever Harlequin books
and ebooks are sold!

And catch up with the previous titles in
The Fortunes of Texas: Digging for Secrets:

Fortune's Baby Claim
by USA TODAY *bestselling author Michelle Major*

Fortune in Name Only
by USA TODAY *bestselling author Tara Taylor Quinn*

Expecting a Fortune
by Nina Crespo

Fortune's Lone-Star Twins
by USA TODAY *bestselling author Teri Wilson*

Worth a Fortune
by Nancy Robards Thompson

Available now!

HARLEQUIN
Reader Service

Enjoyed your book?

Try the perfect subscription for Romance readers and get more great books like this delivered right to your door.

See why over 10+ million readers have tried Harlequin Reader Service.

Start with a Free Welcome Collection with free books and a gift—valued over $20.

Choose any series in print or ebook. See website for details and order today:

TryReaderService.com/subscriptions